DEAD MAN'S PAIN

A man being pursued collides with Nicholas Penn. Assuming his pocket has been pilfered in the scuffle, Nicholas also gives chase. But the stranger fails to see a horse careering down the road, and is trampled by the animal, seemingly mortally. Later, though, Nicholas discovers that the man was no thief — and still lives. Mystified, he is determined to discover the truth behind the 'dead' man's pain . . .

Books by Valerie Holmes
in the Linford Mystery Library:

DEAD TO SIN

VALERIE HOLMES

DEAD MAN'S PAIN

Complete and Unabridged

LINFORD
Leicester

First published in Great Britain

First Linford Edition
published 2017

A catalogue record for this book is available
from the British Library.

ISBN 978–1–4448–3527–4

Published by
F. A. Thorpe (Publishing)
Anstey, Leicestershire

Set by Words & Graphics Ltd.
Anstey, Leicestershire
Printed and bound in Great Britain by
T. J. International Ltd., Padstow, Cornwall

This book is printed on acid-free paper

1

Nicholas Penn pulled at the high collar of his greatcoat so that the pouring rain did not drip down the back of his neck. He hesitated momentarily, staring at the state of the road he was about to cross, debating whether the prospect of the hot meal at the inn opposite would be worth the effort of wading through the muck to get to it. The stink was almost enough to put him off his food, as it was market day and herds of farm animals had already been driven along this high street to sell in the main square.

The distant movement of an approaching horse-drawn carriage caught his eye. The animal seemed skittish, sliding on the filth, unnerved by the torrent. Nicholas stood back, waiting for it to pass.

Guy should have stabled the horse by now. Nicholas looked around for the lad, wondering why he had let him come along. He could have left him with Amelia, but his half-sister's mother had just been declared 'ill of mind' and removed to a safe place where she could not harm anyone. That was enough for Amelia to contend with, he thought, although she had coped well so far. Nicholas could not desert Guy so soon after rescuing him from poverty.

Nick shrugged and tipped his hat so that the water dripped off its brim, only to be knocked sideways by a man rushing past him, striking his shoulder hard. 'Careful!' Nicholas snapped, and felt the man fall against his pocket; he recognised the familiar trick. A much younger Nicholas had once tried such an act himself. His efforts to rescue his mother from the dire circumstances of a debtors' prison where his father had left her had been futile.

'Stop, thief!' a voice was heard shouting further up the high street. Nicholas's response was instantaneous; the bastard must have filched his pocket — his wallet. He saw startled eyes staring wildly back at him; panic spread across the man's face. Nicholas shook his head, clenched his fists and broke into a run.

Heads turned as the thief in the tweed coat took to his heels and the two men raced down the sodden street, slipping, sliding and barging into the people as they went. Most gentlefolk were indoors away from the rain and stench of the day. The traders were already angry enough at the dreadful weather without having a thief to contend with. An upskittled basket of apples caused another angry outcry. Despite the uproar, Nicholas continued relentlessly. The cad glanced back; seeing Nicholas gaining on him, he turned direction, stepping out into the road. He was light of foot and was already at the corner where Rook Street met Upper Lane, but Nicholas was catching up with him quickly. It was then that fate intervened.

Nicholas heard the startled horse's whinny as the driver shouted out an unheeded warning to the thief: 'Get out of the way! Clear ahead!' The coach's brake had no effect in the wet conditions; coupled with an animal ready to bolt, there was naught to be done. The thief, having little time to see what was about to crash into him, could not react. The nervous horse reared. The man had taken a giant leap of faith to escape his pursuers, but had run into the path of the hapless animal.

Nicholas froze. Time seemed to stand still as he witnessed the gut-wrenching crack of hoof, wood and bone mangling, shrouded by a deafening scream of anguish from the fallen man. In Nicholas's mind, all the battle scenes that he had ever witnessed came back to haunt him: the thundering noise of the horse's hooves; the perpetual motion as it darted from one side of the road to the other; the carriage railing, almost upturning, its passenger thrown out of the door to fall into the foul detritus in the middle of the road. A cacophony of shouts and cries went up. The only sounds that were missing were those of gunshots and explosions. Some people went to the aid of the passenger lying in the dirt, cursing the horse, the driver and his bad fortune; some went to the driver as he tried to calm the animal down. Only Nicholas stared down at the pathetic broken figure lying on the ground.

2

Nicholas bent over the man's twisted body and took hold of his wrist, searching for signs of life. He felt a faint pulse and realised the man was not yet dead. Run down by the charging animal, his torso was a mixture of mud and blood. The man was an enigma; his attire was quite hardy and well made, yet he had run off as a thief would, condemning himself by his own actions.

Nicholas had always held a healthy respect for horses; they were beautiful creatures of indeterminate character. He had wanted to serve in the cavalry fighting the French, but had instead been bought a commission serving with his father. He looked around to see what help was available; he saw that the driver was now frantically trying to still the horse. With help, he had steadied it and was now walking it full circle, as other carts and people traversed around the scene of mayhem. Vendors were silenced momentarily. Then the driver's shouts could be heard.

'The bloody fool leapt into the road! What was I to do? He could have broken the horse's leg!' The rain pelted down and the rest of his curses were washed away.

Where the hell was Guy when he needed him? Nicholas realised he could have perhaps done with someone else around to watch his own back. With no authority other than that he was an ex-soldier and knew how to give and take command, he raised his head and barked out an order for someone to find help for the fallen man — a surgeon, he suggested.

'Will I do?' a gruff voice said.

Nicholas looked up and saw a man holding a coat above his head. He was shielding his bloodied apron, which was wrapped around his sturdy girth. Nicholas glanced at his arms and thought, yes, they looked strong and he able. He would do very well.

A young lad skidded to a halt by Nicholas's side. 'Mr Penn! I lost you in this pesky rain and the crowd, but then I heard such a commotion — and did you see that man fly out of that carriage . . . ? Bloody hell!' he gasped as he looked down at the thief's mangled form. 'Sorry, sir! I came as soon as I could, but what happened here, Mr Penn?' The lad was wrinkling his nose up as he stared at the man's body, one leg bent out at an unnatural angle.

Nicholas nodded, acknowledging Guy, but his attention was on the man standing over him. 'Are you a surgeon?' he queried.

'Butcher.' The man winked. 'I did once amputate a man's leg when I was serving.'

'Good. Can we move him quickly?' Nicholas asked, and looked around. No one else seemed to have time or inclination, or show any sign of care for the fellow's situation. He was a thief and had caused unrest; therefore he could no doubt rot in hell until the passenger and horse were safe, in their eyes. More cattle were just appearing on the road approaching the town. 'We need to move him now.'

'Is he dead?' Guy asked.

The butcher guffawed. 'Serves the

bugger right if he is. He won't be running off with honest folks' money no more, that's for sure.' He slipped his arms into his coat and then placed his hands under the man's shoulders, hooking him by his armpits ready to lift him up.

'Near as damn it,' Nicholas said, but he wanted to get him indoors before his passing, and before anyone intervened. 'Help to move him, Guy. Grab his legs.'

The crowd thinned, dispersing fast. A few diligent souls worked to clear the road so that they could get on with their market day and make way for the next batch of animals to be driven into town. The two men helped lift the injured chap into the back of the butcher's shop opposite. It was dark inside, the floor strewn with sawdust and hay that was well-soiled. Carcasses were hung from large hooks from the ceiling racks suspended from strong wooden beams above. Further in, salted pork and beef were lined up along the back wall. The place stank of death. Nicholas knew the smell well; whether man or beast, death was death.

The long slab in the middle of the back

room was fortunately clear. It was wet, as the man had obviously swilled it with water to remove some of the gore from the previous carcass that had adorned it. They placed the thief unceremoniously upon it. Nicholas cradled the man's head in his hand to prevent further bruising by it bouncing against the harsh surface.

The butcher had no such qualms as he took hold of the bent leg and straightened it with one swift, bold move. The man groaned and lurched forward in pain, spitting blood.

'Careful,' Nicholas said.

'He's a lowlife and a thief. Why show care, man?' The words were filled with anger.

Guy stood to the side, taking in every detail of the man's attire. Nicholas knew the lad had an acute eye for detail. 'Because a dead man cannot speak, and I want to know who he is. Even a body should have a name,' Nicholas said, and stared back at the butcher.

'No, sir, they don't; but this one ain't got long, so let's help him speak out quickly. Tongues loosen and words flow more free-like when spoken through a dead man's pain.'

'He's not yet dead!' Nicholas snapped. The man shrugged. 'Guy, empty his pockets out.' Nicholas lowered his head to the man's face. The eyes were shut. 'What's your name, thief?' His voice was calm and even.

The butcher made to grab the man's leg. Nicholas put his hand up. 'No more pain.' He glared at the butcher, and then looked back down. 'You have suffered enough, have you not?' He softened his voice as if soothing a hurt child. 'Tell me, quickly.'

The man's lips slowly opened. 'Not stolen. For Miss Amelia . . . needs it. Hers by right . . . Mother . . . ' He gasped and convulsed.

'It's no use asking for your ma now, man. God, what a coward!' The butcher spat out his words in disgust.

Nicholas ignored him. The man was dying; he could cry for whoever he wished if it helped him.

Guy had removed everything he could find from the man's pockets. The butcher was looking around distractedly. 'Look here, I've a business to run.' He buttoned up his own jacket over his apron. 'I've beasts to buy. You have him out of here by the time I come back, you hear me? I'll tell Dr Sands and ask that word be sent to the parish constable, and you can pay the coin to have him seen to and removed. They'll find a hole to put him in soon enough.'

Nicholas nodded. Surrounded by hung, salted meat on long hooks, this was one hell of a place to die. 'For whom?' he asked the injured man softly.

The man croaked, and spittle drooled from his mouth; his jaw sagged, but words could no longer escape.

Nicholas quickly looked through the items in Guy's hands. He found a purse — not his, though. Slipping his hand into his own pocket, he realised that his own coin had not been stolen. The money that was on the man would be enough to pay for his treatment or passing. There was also a pipe, and a small pistol with *THR* engraved on the handle, but nothing that would give the man a name of his own. He had not stolen anything from him. In fact, Nicholas found that a soft pouch had been slipped into his own coat. He was about to remove it to disclose what was kept inside when two men burst in.

'Stand back! This man is a thief. I would have him speak!' a large man shouted. Guy flinched and took a step behind Nicholas.

Nicholas looked down at the defenceless stranger. Guilt and regret swept through him as he realised that his part in the pursuit had driven this man, who had stolen nothing from him, to risk his life in his escape. 'You will need to make your demands to a higher order, then. He is beyond earthly words now.' He stepped away.

Brusquely, the man came forward, brushing past Nicholas, and rifled through the body's pockets, stripping away bloody garments in pursuit of his goal. 'Where are his things?' His eyes turned to Guy, who was standing next to a small stool upon which the dead man's effects had been laid down. 'Them his?' the man asked.

Guy nodded. The second strode forward, and both eagerly grabbed the purse. Then they rifled further, pulling off the man's boots; nothing was to be found there either.

'What, pray, do you seek?' Nicholas asked them, anger rising with their lack of respect of the person whose fresh corpse they affronted. The man could be no more than thirty years of age. To be dealt with in such a manner seemed wrong. His clothes were of fair quality, and his body seemed healthy — or had been, but now he was no more than rags and broken bones.

'He was a cutpurse. We seek what is ours. Thomas Henry Root. Gentry fallen low in the gambling dens of York. You take anything from him, boy?' he asked Guy, then grabbed him by the scruff whilst the other man frisked him abruptly.

Nicholas moved forward. 'Leave him!' he demanded. 'The boy is my ward. Now if you are done here, I will leave you to report his demise.'

Guy side-stepped, then skirted the hung corpses to follow Nicholas out into the rain and away from the stench within.

'What's your name?' the man shouted to him.

Nicholas did not look back, but instead walked purposefully along the road.

'Mr Penn, wait, please. Aren't we stopping?' Guy asked as he ran alongside him. 'Why are we going this way? The inn's over there.' He pointed back along the road. Holding his coat tight with his other hand, rain dripping from the peak of his cap, he looked wretched.

'Because, Guy, we are not staying here. I have lost my appetite and I now have business to see to.'

'But . . . but . . . it's wet and cold, and what of our food? You must eat, or you'll be ill.' He stopped. 'I haven't lost my appetite . . . Sir?'

Nicholas quickened his pace.

'Mr Penn!' Guy pleaded.

Nicholas did not stop. He was livid. He had made a bad mistake by joining in the chase. He wanted to find a new life and not be dogged at the heels by death. Now he would try to make some amends for his poor judgement. He spun around and stared down at Guy. He saw the boy shrink back.

The shop further along sold pies. He

opened its door and bought some freshly made ones. He asked for them to be well wrapped, and also stopped long enough to buy a bottle of ale. With them carefully cradled against his body, they made for the church. The market square, with all its trade and miserable animals, was at the opposite end of the town.

Nicholas and Guy slipped inside the Norman building and took shelter discreetly on a well-used pew at the back of the building. 'Here.' He smiled at the boy and handed him his pie, which was gratefully accepted. At least one of them still had an appetite for life.

3

Guy looked up after he had eagerly sated his hunger and thirst. Nicholas returned his stare; the boy reminded him of himself at the same age — roughly eleven, he guessed. He still took every bite as if it was going to be his last meal for ages. Nicholas remembered being that hungry himself once, and was grateful it was no more than a distant memory, even if it did still haunt him. He sighed. He was wet, but glad to be out of the rain. The church was quite dark inside. The candles were unlit. Perhaps, he thought, the inclement weather had stopped the clergy or keepers from coming out to do their duty. Straw had been thrown on the stones inside to act as a mop for whatever was walked into the sacred building.

Why had he come? He glanced at the altar, and the coloured window behind that pictured the Saviour, and sighed again. He had come here as it was a place of peace, and he still searched to find that place within himself. Today he had witnessed a death, an unnecessary death. It seemed as if it dogged his path. Yet, looking at the young lad whose care he had taken on to avoid him being half-starved and abandoned, he had at least tried to save one soul. His own seemed lost for now, and he had been presented with another mystery to solve.

'Why did you leave so quick, Mr Penn?' Guy enquired, breaking across his thoughts.

'Because of this.' He pulled the velvet pouch from his pocket and held it low so that it could not be seen above the pews should anyone else enter.

'What is it?' Guy asked, his eyes taking in every detail.

It had initials embroidered upon it in gold thread. Nicholas admired the workmanship. Set against the deep russet colour of the pouch, they stood out, looking very grand. The initials were *EB*.

'Well, it certainly does not stand for 'Amelia'.'

'Strange, as you have a sister called that,' Guy commented.

'Yes, it is; but no more than a coincidence, I am sure. It is a common enough name.'

'Who is the Miss Amelia it's meant for, then?'

'That I do not know.' Nicholas turned it over in his hand and then upended it so that a gold-coloured key slipped out onto his palm. The end had an unusual shape to it. It reminded Nicholas of a tap-room key, but this was smaller and more refined. He shook his head and flipped the key over in his hand. No mark had been made upon it. It was plain as plain could be, yet quite heavy and solidly made.

'Maybe them men knew who she was.' Guy looked at it and then into Nicholas's eyes. 'I wouldn't trust them, though. They were real bruisers if ever I saw any. Don't think they were proper gents like you, despite their fine clothes.' Guy looked around at the church. 'Often wondered what them windows looked like on the inside. Grand, eh?' He smiled, then looked thoughtful. The lad glanced to the ceiling and swallowed. 'Do you think He minds me being in here?'

Nicholas laughed. 'Oh, I think He'd be delighted, Guy.' He nodded his agreement about the two men. 'I think you're right — they were 'bruisers'. But why were they after him? And what's that key for?' He did not correct Guy's misconception that the men had been dressed like gentlemen. To Guy, their jackets and trousers matched, so that made them rich; but to Nicholas's more experienced eyes, they were clearly men of a hardy trade. However, the boy was certainly a good judge of character.

Nicholas had no intention of becoming a thief himself, but the key had been given to him. The message had been that of a dying man; and whoever Amelia was, he needed to find her and decide if this truly was hers. She could also be in danger, as her dead friend had obviously been. He had a couple of names to begin his search with: Thomas Henry Root, Amelia, and the initials *EB*.

His temper cooled, and he realised how foolhardy his decision to move on immediately was. 'I'll pay for a room here tonight. It's too wet and hard going to travel further today. Plus, we need to dry out and warm through. But tomorrow we shall leave.' He placed the key back into its pouch and put it in his inside pocket, one that was safely tucked away from passing, prying hands.

'Can I stay in your room?' Guy asked.

Nicholas stared at him. 'I'm hardly going to make you sleep with the horse!'

Guy smiled. 'Thanks; you really are a friend, sir.'

Nicholas ignored this declaration and instead thought about his next move. The men had said Root was in debt in York, so that might be where he would head to next. He knew a man there who might be able to help him. Was he too proud to go and ask that particular gentleman for information? Nicholas pondered.

Wilson Pendleton had rented a house on the outskirts of York for himself and his daughter — Nicholas's half-sister, Amelia — to stay. Wilson had kept his word to Amelia; he had promised that her mother would receive the care she needed in comfortable surroundings. Wilson's wife, Elizabeth, needed a keeper to protect the good name of his family and Amelia's reputation, and to keep her from the people she hated. Elizabeth despised Nicholas, Wilson's illegitimate son.

Guy smiled as if he had had a sudden inspiration. 'Would Mister Pendleton know of him?'

Nicholas looked at Guy and did not answer for a moment, wondering if the boy had some secret power to read his mind. Then he blinked as if taken aback by his own stupidity at giving such superstitious nonsense any credence at all and stood up. 'Perhaps,' he answered, and walked off, lost in his thoughts.

If only Wilson, his father, had shown more respect for his superiors and less foolhardy bravery in battle, he could still have held his rank and place in the army, which had been his life. Not content to have any stain on his record (having been accused of shooting a rival on the field), he had made one daring decision too many; as a result, he had lost men, temporarily lost possession of their flag, and had come home retired, commission sold, rather than face further investigation and possible disgrace. Yet still, he swore he had been wronged — an order incorrectly passed on by a fool of a major who had better connections than he. So Wilson had privately taken the fall.

Nicholas shared both his name and his bad blood, and was another rising soldier showing daring upon the field. His term of service had also been curtailed. Better to rid the ranks of the rot before he cost men's lives also. It was a bitter pill for Nicholas to swallow, and he had hated his father for it. By his blood he had been condemned, and had also had his hand forced to sell his commission. Both then had the choice between desk jobs or returning to their lives as gentlemen. Nicholas had decided to cut loose on returning to England. He travelled as Nicholas Penn, and had left his father to wallow in his own self-made midden, until a call for help had brought them back together. Nicholas had still found it hard to be in the company of his father and pay the man his due respect, but Fate had intervened. Murders had been committed and, between them, the culprit had been caught. Now this had happened.

★   ★   ★

He entered the dusky room of the inn, Guy following closely behind. People stood cheek by jowl around the bar and the fire. The settles and chairs were not in sufficient numbers to accommodate all the strangers who had arrived for market day and who had ended up sheltering from the downpour. Consequently, the smoky air was moist and stale.

'Ale, mister?' a wench shouted to him above the noise of the banter.

'Room,' he shouted back.

'This way.' She gestured to him to follow her and headed over towards the back of the room, where a wooden stairway led up to a rickety upper floor. She walked to the end of the dark corridor, the floorboards creaking under the weight of each step. She flung open a door to a pokey bedroom. 'This room is eight pennies if you wants your own bed, or six pennies if you shares the bed with another traveller.'

'I'll have my own bed, thank you.' He looked into the sparse room and stared at what looked like a bed with a straw-filled mattress upon which were folded faded sheets and woollen blankets. A chair, table and chamber pot were the only items provided. He stepped inside and Guy went to follow.

'You is charged double for sharing the room with folks you come with — you is two, after all. And it's another sixpence if you wants more blankets . . . '

Nicholas held out a coin. 'That's a shilling. He sleeps on the blanket on the floor. Please send up another one.'

'I've a business to run, you know.' She placed her hands on her hips, and Nicholas saw Guy staring as her bosoms wobbled with the gesture; they looked dangerously near to spilling out from the neckline of her cotton blouse.

'Very well; but if you want people to speak well of it, I would suggest that you make your guests feel both welcome and comfortable.' He smiled at her and took out a sixpence, holding it in the air. 'What do you know of the man who was run over in the street opposite this afternoon?' He dropped the coins into her hand.

'He was a thief. Shame, nice-looking, but he'd been acting oddly. Was in here earlier in the day until them two chaps what he wronged turned up.' She shook her head.

'Was he a regular?' Nicholas persisted.

'Not really. I was thinking earlier, he'd been in a few months back. Then he was happy. On his way to meet his betrothed, he'd said. He was hoping to win a lady's heart. A proper dreamer, he sounded like. How the mighty fall, eh?' She looked at Nicholas as if giving him carefully chosen words of wisdom to heed.

'Who was she?'

'No idea. He was drunk, and talking all pretty and muddled. But no one would have remembered him at all had it not been for the way he returned here. He seemed to have his future all planned out. He's wasted it now. Shame, eh . . . ' she said, smiled, and turned toward the door. 'I'll send the lass up to set you a fire and bring a blanket for the lad, sir.' She smiled, and then paused. 'Them men were mighty angry when Dr Sands insisted his family be told of the accident. Soon as they knew he had family, they left in all that rain, no charges made against him, no word sent to the magistrate, no nothing — strange, eh?'

'Strange indeed. Who were the men?'

'No idea, sir. No names given, no questions answered, just asked.'

'Where is his family? I would like to pay my respects.'

'Don't know that either,' she said as she stepped outside the room, pocketing her coins. 'You best see Dr Sands. He'll be in his rooms by noon tomorrow. He'll talk to the likes of you, sir. He'll know. I'll send up some warm water for you to wash in.'

'Thank you,' Nicholas replied as he closed the door.

'Do I have to sleep on the floor, sir? I could curl up small on the chair and you'd not know I was there.' Guy's hopeful face stared back at him.

Nicholas looked at his soulful eyes and shrugged. He hung up his wet coat on the peg by the door and told Guy to do the same. A good fire was lit, and soon the room was warm.

Nicholas studied the key again. It was, he suspected, the item that would unlock the truth. But it was a mystery in itself. So who was Amelia, and why had Root been running from those two ruffians? Whyever would he have placed it in the pocket of a stranger — unless he'd been desperate for it not to be found on him? He must have expected to be able to retrieve it at some point.

He placed it back in the inside pocket of his waistcoat, which he intended to keep on him. The pouch would have made it too bulky, so he used that to place a couple of loose coins in and left it in his coat pocket. Tomorrow he would go to see this Dr Sands and find out what the doctor knew of the dead man's past.

4

Guy did not mind being told what to do; he had had a lifetime of being ordered about. Now each day that dawned offered new experiences. Mr Penn was good to him, fed him, and even let him sleep comfy in a chair, wrapped in a blanket by a warm fire. Nicholas had risen early, giving him strict instructions before he left. He was to check on the horse to make sure it had been well tended. Guy had worked as a stable lad for his meagre board after his mother died. Nicholas had insisted that he stay out of people's way, and return to their room to wait for him after he'd paid a visit to Dr Sands.

Yet Guy was used to wandering around the town he had been brought up in, being invisible and watching the world as it passed him by. He would check the animal first and then explore this new town before they moved on again. Travelling was something he was beginning to enjoy. He had already journeyed from Gorebeck, passing its surrounding fields, moors and woods, to the vast whaling port of Whitby. It had teemed with people, vessels, fish, and ships on the horizon going back and forth from London to Newcastle, Mr Penn had told him, and other places in between that sounded so foreign to him. The world, he was realising, was a vast place, and he wanted to see more of it. So Guy set to exploring.

* * *

Nicholas arrived at the house of Dr Sands. It was a new construction with columns at the side of its black-painted door, which was crowned by a semi-circular fanlight above. He was a man who was obviously successful.

The door was opened by a manservant who took his card and led him into a small waiting room at the rear of the building. The narrow space was lined with ash and elm spindle-backed chairs. The rush seats looked worn but practical. He seated himself, trying to frame the words he would use to explain his interest in the dead man. However, the key would remain his secret for now.

The door reopened some twenty minutes later. 'This way, sir,' the servant said.

Nicholas followed him to the doctor's room. The window of small panels of glass allowed daylight to fall onto his neatly organised desk; at the side was a simple chair. Against the wall to his right as he entered was a single cot bed, raised to waist height, with a crisp unstained starched white linen sheet stretched upon it. A bookcase behind him next to the door proudly sported some impressive titles, no doubt from his scholarly Oxbridge days. The man finished writing something, placed his pen back on the rest by the inkwell, and stood. He pulled on his jacket, covering his white shirt and black waistcoat, and gestured to Nicholas to take a seat in the chair. All was orderly, all was immaculate, and Nicholas sensed that something here was very strange.

'Now, my good man, what brings you here outside of my normal hours? You are indeed fortunate I arose early this morning to complete my letters.' He looked at Nicholas through round, metal-framed eye-glasses. 'Speak boldly, and in confidence, as there is nothing I have not seen or treated in my years.' He smiled at Nicholas, who began to realise that Dr Sands was more than a mere country doctor. He appeared to be not just a man who had studied books, watched lectures and collected his license; this man he felt knew his trade. But he was immaculate, as was his surgery — almost to the point of looking new . . . and unused.

'I am grateful for your time, but I do not ail. I come here as I witnessed an accident yesterday, and I would ask if you could tell me who the dead man was.' Nicholas tried to sound curiously innocent, and show he was purely concerned about the events and the man's horrendous demise.

'Mr Smythe was muddied, bruised and indeed irate, but he is fine and back in his home as we speak.' The doctor paused. 'Do you wish a note of introduction? I know the family well.' He raised a quizzical brow.

'No, Dr Sands, it is not he of whom I speak; for I heard him voice his opinions after he was ejected from the vehicle, and knew instantly he was well enough. It is the man who was struck down by the horse and carriage.' Nicholas watched as the doctor removed his spectacles and sat back in his chair.

'Then I am pleased to inform you that the man of whom you speak is not dead, sir.'

Nicholas could not contain his surprise. 'But he was . . . he seemed . . . he was . . . crushed . . . ' He ran the events through his mind, replaying the scene. His leg certainly was badly broken. There had been blood from his mouth. His body was bruised.

'I found him with two men who took to their heels as soon as I arrived. I thought they were meaning to rob him, but his few belongings were left on a stool in the most humbling of circumstances. It would appear that I disturbed them, as they had rifled through his garments in a very ungainly fashion. His leg is lost to him from below the knee. His chest carried the mark of a hoof, and will do for some time; and his ribs were bruised and cracked. His jaw is also in need of treatment. He is not a well man; but if God is willing, he may one day talk and walk again. I hope that allays your concern.' He replaced his glasses upon his face and reached for his pen.

'Could I see him?'

'There would be little point in that. He is indeed incapacitated, and is sleeping as the pain is quite intense. If his amputation site heals, and his jaw, he needs time, rest and care. I do not advise visitors. You understand he has been through enough.'

He picked up his pen once more. Nicholas knew his time there had been politely ended. He stood up. 'It is indeed good of you to take such care of a man who has been shouted down as a thief.'

Dr Sands leaned back in his chair; his portly figure seemed somewhat rounder. Nicholas sensed that he did not take well to being questioned. The man was not a simple country doctor who charged around his patients' houses on horseback, but one who had a carriage, was well respected, and no doubt had had many a free meal from his richer patients. So why did he take such interest in a fallen man who had gambling debts and an uncertain lifestyle?

'I think you misheard, sir. Mr Root is the child of the Roots of Middleham. He is their only son, and stands to inherit their vast estate.' He paused. 'I am a man of medicine. I seek to heal the wounded and injured,' he concluded humbly.

'His father must be devastated,' Nicholas replied.

'As any man would be. Good day, sir.' The man returned to his writing. Nicholas, dismissed, left.

*   *   *

Guy slipped behind the newer buildings that housed the doctor's office. He did not want Mr Penn to see him and think he was untrustworthy after having being told to stay at the inn. It was just that he wanted to feel free to roam at will for a while longer.

He cut down an alleyway that led to a

walk along the path beside the river. Ahead, a barge was just moving off on the water. He slowed long enough for it to move away from the bank. Two men manoeuvred it downstream, and then Guy continued walking by. He glanced back, and for a moment caught the eye of one of the men who was staring at him, but then had to focus on the water's flow. Guy quickened his step: he knew those eyes, and they had accused him of stealing in the back room of the butcher's shop. Seeing that he was signalling for his friend to take the barge back to the bank, Guy ran toward the main street. He should have listened to Mr Penn. Freedom only brought him trouble. He was better staying close to his gentleman friend. Then, one day, he would be able to stand safe in his own fine shoes.

* * *

Nicholas left the meeting feeling very uneasy. He could have sworn that Root had died. Good God, had his judgement become so dulled since he had left the army? He looked at his fob watch and decided that Guy could wait a while longer. At least the lad would be safe inside the inn. He went instead to the butcher's where the body had lain. Or, rather, where the poor chap had been deserted to his fate.

'You again!' the gruff voice said, and then his arm fell as he cleaved a carcass.

'Ah, I'm flattered that you remember me.' Nicholas smiled at the butcher, whose skill with the knife was deft.

'Not every day a man replaces a beast on my slab. What can I do for you?' He glanced up.

'The two men who were here yester-day . . . '

'What two men?' the butcher asked, but continued working.

'When you returned, were they still here? Has the parish constable been to see you?'

Nicholas watched as he slowly placed the knife down and wiped his hands on his grubby, blood-stained apron. 'You ask a lot of questions, Mr Penn. Why?' He folded his arms.

'Just wondered.' Nicholas puzzled about how he knew his name, but then remembered that Guy had called to him on arriving yesterday.

The butcher stared directly at him. 'You can't con an old soldier so easily, sir. There was no constable, no men, and no body. Just a few coins left on that there stool, which I took to be for me trouble and the use of me slab. So did he just get up and walk away? Tell me, did I miss out on a miracle? He didn't look like he was going to walk anywhere when I left you, mister. So you tell me why you are asking Malachi so many questions. Who are you?' He leaned back against a bench, and watched and waited for Nicholas to reply.

Nicholas nodded; this man saw the truth of it. 'I am confused, and I thought you might be able to help clarify a few points. I have just spoken to the doctor, and, well, it seems that the man still lives.'

The butcher raised his eyebrows. His bald head seemed to accentuate the gesture. 'Bloody hell! I had a miracle in me own shop and missed it. There's no justice left in this world, is there?'

Nicholas shrugged. 'The man was as near death as could be judged by the human eye. I'm no doctor, but . . . '

'But you seen it plenty. You've served, sir, haven't you?'

Nicholas agreed.

'Your hands are not those of a prissy gent. They've worked — but not at a trade, I'd wager. Now, to answer your questions, there was no one living nor dead here when I returned. The parish constable has been nowhere near. So if you want to ask questions, go to see him, Mr Jacob Battle. You'll find him in the Rabbit and Hare in the old part of town. I don't know what happened, and I make it my business not to ask too many questions. If the good doctor has told you what's what, then I'd accept his word for it. He's respected here.'

'His patients come to him?'

'You don't let up, do you?' Malachi shrugged and glanced out of his open doorway, then ambled casually over to it. Seemingly satisfied that there was no one within earshot, he wandered back to Nicholas, who was trying not to breathe too deeply as that ominous smell of death hung heavy in the air. 'Listen, sir, this town has two doctors. One has a house on the outskirts; he gets up early, visits folk in his small battered gig — or on horseback if the road's no good — and comes home late. His name is Pearce. He's a young lad, but ordinary folk speak well of him. Then we have the educated and stately Dr Sands, who has them come to him. He dines well, stays at houses here and there, and supports the home for the injured soldiers on the outskirts of town. The Haven — fanciful name, but many say that is what it is: a place of peace. If he said the man rose and walked on water, then folk will say they saw it happen. Now I have a business that sells meat to them poor folks in The Haven and the local gentry, so whilst I still have a livelihood, could you ask your questions elsewhere?'

Nicholas nodded. 'Thank you,' he said, and put his hand in his purse to offer the man some coin.

The butcher shook his head. 'Free advice, one old soldier to a young one.

Make sure you live to be old, eh,' he added quietly, and then hacked the carcass clean in two.

Nicholas stood away from the splash of blood and left. Remembering Guy, he decided he had better collect him before the boy gave in to a desire to explore the place for himself, and then Nicholas would ask his questions elsewhere.

★ ★ ★

Guy paused for breath as he reached the high street, which ran down the centre of the town. He had seen one of the men leap off the barge to the bank as the other secured it once more. His breath and fear deepened, as he could be certain one would give chase behind him — but where had the other one cut through to? The market square was cleared of pens, although the mess remained. The rain had stopped, but the water lay in puddles and runnels everywhere. This had kept respectable folk indoors.

He relaxed when he could see the inn in the distance, and made his way across the road. Glancing back, he saw one of the two men on the other side. It was definitely one of his pursuers, but he seemed in no hurry to cross and follow him. Instead he folded his arms and smiled. Guy felt uneasy. Where was the other one — still with the barge, perhaps? He soon found out. Out of the inn stepped the second bruiser. Behind him was a man in a distinctive uniform — the pressgang was in town! Guy turned and ran as fast as he could, but a hand grabbed him and swung him round, then dragged him through a doorway. Momentarily confused by the dimness of the light, he soon realised where he was as he remembered the smell instantly.

'This way!' The butcher bundled him into his shop, down a hatch, and the next thing Guy knew as he fell into a dark storage space was the noise of a barrel or something heavy been dragged across the trapdoor above him. He swallowed. Why could he not have stayed in the room like he had been told to by Mr Penn? Fearful, he curled up into a ball and waited.

5

Nicholas returned to the room ready to collect Guy and his bag and head off to the Rabbit and Hare to find Mr Jacob Battle, the parish constable. If the accident had not been reported, then Nicholas wanted to know why not. However, the lad was not there.

He hung his coat on the door peg and left his things, deciding to seek out the woman who had rented him the room; perhaps she had softened and decided to feed Guy. The lad had a way with him that seemed to win over the hearts of serving wenches. He smiled; it would no doubt get him in and out of more bother than enough as he grew up. He saw her at the counter as he stepped out of the stairwell.

'Have you seen my ward?' he asked her, noting the way she slammed down a jug of porter when she heard his voice.

'He left shortly after you did, sir.' She

turned to face him, crossing her arms under her ample bosom. 'And it was just as well for him that he did so. The pressgang is in town. They've hit us after a market day when the weather is bad, so folk are still here! People are trying to eke out a meagre living from their labour, on a day when the younger hands would be helping to bring in the herds and flocks to sell. The bastards! They usually keep to the coast and take seafaring folk, not farmers!'

'Did he return here?' Nicholas reached into his pocket for a few coins.

'Nope, he slipped out as if no one would notice — but I always do, and he has not been back since.' She winked. 'It pays to stay alert, as some would slip by without settling their dues, or at least try to.'

Nicholas looked around him. The room was nearly empty except for a few older locals who were seated on the upturned barrels smoking clay pipes, drinking, and scowling in his general direction.

'That's why folk is scarce here today. Word spreads real quick-like. They won't stay long, for people start getting together, preparing to fight to reclaim their kin. They've taken two lads off the land, poor sods. One is needed to support his ma and her nest of bairns. Hope your friend keeps his head down, or you'll not see him again for dust.' Her mouth was set in a hard line, her ruddy cheeks flushed. She turned away to fill some jars with porter.

'He isn't old enough to be pressed,' Nicholas said. He also felt disgusted at the thought of such a lad being thrown into the violent world of a man of war.

'Then you try to tell them that. He would be a man grown by the time he returned to these shores — that's if he ever did. Then who would know him? He'd be as hard as them, or broken in spirit if not in body. You best find him quickly. They rarely quibble with a gentleman such as you, sir, but then they'll have him away downriver and off on a ship before folk can put up a proper defence. It's us poor folk whose kin they snatch.' She slammed a jug down hard, slopping some of its contents onto the counter as it landed. A splash caught his coat, but she made no apology. He saw the loathing in her eyes, and also felt the same from those few older men who were still in the inn around him. He made to place his coins down on the counter.

She shook her head. 'No, thank you all the same. I don't want that. You give it to the lad when you find him. Mabel doesn't want blood money on her hands. You just pay your dues, and when you find him, leave. I don't want them back here looking for him — or you, for that matter. We've a living to make.'

Nicholas nodded, replaced his coin and left, cursing the lad for his stupid disobedience and his own folly for trusting him to stay put.

* * *

Nicholas searched up and down the high street. He saw a ramshackle group of sailors preparing to leave the town at the far end of the road. Women were jeering and shouting at them as they walked off, swinging clubs in their hands as if to warn the locals not to try anything. Two young lads were in the middle of the group, but not Guy, to Nicholas's relief. If Guy had not been taken, then Nicholas still needed to know where he was, but he could hardly go up to them and ask if they had seen him.

'Damnation!' Nicholas cursed his decision to allow the boy to come with him. If he found him again, he would deliver him to Amelia promptly and insist that he be found a place where he could be taught some proper lessons and discipline. His anger was driving him to make such rash promises and decisions, but underneath he knew that the truth was more personal. He wanted Guy to be safe, to grow and have a future that was not as bleak as his past had been, not to be broken like so many were. Too many lives were being destroyed during this time of war. It had gone on far too long.

'Soldier, you want to help me retrieve someone who has been stolen from the bosom of their family, and in so doing help the lad you came to town with?' a familiar voice asked.

Nicholas turned to see the butcher standing behind him. 'You know where he is?' he asked.

'I may have a very good notion where he is being kept — likely out of harm's way. But, if I return him safely to you, then I would make one thing clear, Mr Penn: I want my nephew safe also.' He gestured with his head up the road to the departing pressgang. 'His ma needs him, and also his friend needs to stay where he can grow strong working on the land his father has tilled before him. Now, you can ride up as bold as brass and try demanding their return, begging for their compassion as their mothers have, but I don't think you'll convince them to hand the lads over. They won't give him or his friend up easy. Or, you can help an old soldier and do what we do best — beat the enemy at their own game. Are you willing to go skirmishing, sir?' The man stared him straight in the eye.

'Are you seriously attempting to hold Guy to ransom, or are you asking my help as a 'friend' in a time of need?' Nicholas glared back. He was in no mood to be coerced, but he did feel as though he was being drawn into another act of charity.

'No, sir. I wouldn't attempt such a stupid act, as you only have to report me, and my business and family are done for. But if it hadn't been for my quick thinking, your lad would be with them now. He was being watched by a couple of strangers. I think they set the pressgang on his tail. So you both appear to be in need of a genuine friend who knows this place, and one who will watch your back. I'll show you where he is, and then we'll hand him to Mabel to keep with her until we return. He needs to learn to stay where he is put. Then, if we don't return, he'll have a life helping out at the inn.'

'Very well.' Nicholas nodded, knowing how pleased Mabel would be at Guy being returned to her care. But it would inevitably teach the lad a lesson he needed to learn. He must learn to obey orders. He could not see Guy settling for a life in an inn again, but then Nicholas had every intention of returning. He had one mystery to solve already, and was a trained soldier; the navy held no threat to him.

They made for the butcher's shop. Nicholas's fists were clenched by his side, ready should an attack be imminent. The barrel was dragged back, the trapdoor lifted, and he stared into the hole where Guy was cowering in the corner. The boy sprang to his feet, eager to climb back out.

'Come on, lad,' Nicholas said, and held an arm down so that Guy could pull himself up.

Guy looked shaken. 'Don't like rats! They was trying to eat me alive!' he snapped at the butcher whilst he tried to adjust his eyes to the light again as he was pulled free of the hole. Then he sheepishly looked up at Nicholas. 'Sorry, Mr Penn; I should have returned to the room. I went for a walk to get some air, and then those two bruisers brought the barge back to the bank when they saw me!' He brushed the dirt off his new clothes and glared at the owner of the shop.

'You should be thanking him, not scowling at him,' Nicholas said. 'The pressgang nearly found you.'

Guy's mouth fell open. He had seen the uniforms, knew what they meant, but hearing how near he came to losing his new life hit him hard.

The butcher nodded. 'Yes, lad, the press-gang! Now, you're to stay with Mabel and do as you're told for once. Your Mr Penn and I have some unfinished business, and we don't want you clucking around and getting into bother.' The man met Guy's glare and stared him down. Guy looked at Nicholas for confirmation that this was what he was expected to do.

'You go to our room and stay with my things. Be ready to move when I come back if necessary — but Guy, don't wander off again.'

'Yes, Mr Penn,' he answered humbly, and walked to the doorway.

'Guy,' Nicholas asked, 'what barge did you refer to?'

'They was moving one off from the bank at the back of them new houses, until they saw me. Not a big one — the barge, that is — but that's where they come from. He recognised me, and that was when they came back.'

50

Nicholas looked to Malachi, who shrugged. 'Goods are often brought up the river, but I have never seen their faces around here before.'

'Go on, Guy, and tell the wench I will settle up with her when I return.'

'Yes, Mr Penn.' Guy touched the tip of his cap and then left.

'Thank you,' Nicholas said as he acknowledged that the man had risked a lot should he have been found hiding Guy, either by the navy or by the two men who hounded his tracks.

'Thank me when our job is done. I have friends who would help us if asked, but if we go in and spill blood, they will never be able to return to their homes. I need someone with brains as well as brawn.' He laughed at Nicholas's expression. 'I'll provide the brawn, man; you figure out how we can get the lads out of trouble without causing a situation that will end up with arrests or impressments.'

Nicholas looked at him and smiled. 'That's all you want of me, is it?'

The butcher nodded.

6

Guy returned to the inn, surprised to be greeted by receiving a big hug from Mabel. She grabbed hold of his arm, led him behind her counter and sat him down on a small keg behind the serving hatch. 'Are they still after you?' Her eyes scanned the door as if she expected the sailors to burst through it waving their clubs.

'No, ma'am; the butcher, Malachi, hid me, and then sent me here to stay with you until he and Mr Penn returned from their mission to get back his nephew. They've gone after him and his friend,' Guy whispered.

'Praise the Lord!' she declared, and busied herself pouring him a tankard of ale and cutting a slice of ham and bread. 'You is a lucky lad, if ever I met one!' Mabel stared at him. 'You keep down low until your guardian returns for you. If Malachi trusts him, then I may have judged him ill, but I'll not be able to keep you hidden from that pressgang if their plan goes awry. They'll search the town if any one of them gets shot.' She served another customer, and Guy was happy to stay warm, safe and fed for now.

When she had finished, she sank to her haunches next to him. 'When you've eaten that, then you go on up to the room and stay out of sight. If the press return, I'll have old Ned begin playing his flute. It's a way of giving out a warning.' She winked, and then with a grunt at the effort of rising, stood straight.

'Yes, ma'am,' Guy answered, and he smiled sweetly at her, seeing how Mabel had flushed slightly when he called her 'ma'am' again.

⋆　⋆　⋆

Nicholas and Malachi, armed with their pistols, skirted the edge of the forestry shadowing the road and the path of the pressgang. Malachi said he had been told by a farmer that they had a boat moored further upstream. The two men cut across a loop of wooded land to make up time and reach it first as the road followed the water's meander. A narrow track used by the locals cut through the dense undergrowth, not easy to see by a passerby. 'It's a good place for a run,' Malachi explained, referring to the distribution of contraband that was periodically brought up from the coast. Halfway along it were the overgrown ruins of an old abbey, long since forgotten; the once-grand building had housed an order of reclusive monks in the days before it had been ruined by the old King Henry's men.

Once the boat became visible, Malachi tapped Nicholas's shoulder. 'They'll be upon us in about twenty minutes. We can't ambush six men on our own. They'll recognise us for sure. Even if we surprised them and freed the lads, they'd have us hunted down. If we shoot from here, they only have to grab one of them and we'd be lost.' A note of frustration filtered into his voice as Malachi listed the only options that he could see as remotely viable, which were anything but, when thought through properly.

'We are not going to shoot or ambush anyone. We are going for the boat,' Nicholas said, and raised a butcher's cleaver that he had been carrying in his left hand. 'Or, to be more precise, I am.'

'You're going to sink it?' Malachi looked confused for the first time since Nicholas had met him.

'Not so obvious as that. Stay here and watch my back.' Nicholas ran down the bank to the boat. He worked quickly. Leaving his boots on the bank, he waded into the river's shallows. With a few deft blows he managed to damage the bottom of the boat, splintering the wood so that it began a slow leak. Satisfied, he jumped back to the bank and unfastened its moorings, giving it a firm push, letting the current slowly drift it off into the river's course. Pleased that it was free of the reeds, he grabbed his boots and made his way back to the cover of the woods, diving into its shadows, quickly pulling his precious polished boots onto his wet feet.

Minutes later, the group of sailors was seen approaching along the road. Nicholas and Malachi watched silently

55

and waited as the two men at the front gave a shout that the boat was loose. The group of men instantly split up. Four went forward whilst two stayed to guard their victims in the shelter of the woodland. Two of the four then dropped their weapons onto the bank and started wading into the water, swimming as they were soon out of their depths. The other two stayed on the bank, looking around them for any sign of an attack, whilst monitoring their colleagues' progress with pistols and clubs at the ready. Watching their companions, they were soon distracted, as the two sailors swam further into the river to retrieve the vessel; one grabbed the rope and started swimming it back to the men on the land who now waded in to meet him.

'It's letting in water!' shouted the sailor who was heaving himself over the side of the boat. He started to bail it out with his hands.

All four were now totally absorbed in their task of saving the vessel that they so desperately needed to return to their ship, the job made more difficult as it was now taking in water at a quicker rate than the man could empty it on his own.

Nicholas and Malachi made their way to the edge of the woodland. Nicholas picked up a rock and hurled it with all his might at a tree in front of the small group. Heads instantly turned to the direction of the cracking noises it made as it struck a branch and then fell through the leaves to the undergrowth below. Without a word being exchanged between the two ex-soldiers, they sprang forward, flooring the two sailors. Malachi had knocked his man senseless and was instantly cutting the lads' hands free. Both took to their heels, heading for the safety of the trees they knew so well.

Nicholas had more of a struggle on his hands, as he was fighting a seasoned sailor who was as strong as two, and angry as hell. The man spun around and struck out his fist, catching the line of Nicholas's jaw. If Nicholas's reactions had not been so quick, he would have been out cold; the force of the blow was avoided, but he had been wrong-footed, and fell to the sodden earth. It was then the sailor grabbed the butcher's cleaver Nicholas had dropped, and raised it high — but instead of landing his blow, the sailor fell to Nicholas's side, the cleaver falling inches from his brow. Nicholas, eyes widened in the realisation that his skull had nearly been halved, shook for a moment. Malachi stood behind him. He had not run with his nephew but had stayed and fought, striking the man to save Nicholas from death or capture.

There was no time for thanks or gratitude. Malachi collected his cleaver and helped pull a shaken Nicholas to his feet as they both stumbled back into the cover of the trees. A gunshot was heard overhead, but it was too far off to be accurate or a threat to them.

They ran, and kept running until they found the narrow path that would return them to the shelter of the ruins of the old abbey hidden deep within the heart of the woodland.

'They'll never find you here, lads,' Malachi told the two frightened young men, slapping both heartily on their backs. 'I'll send supplies and we'll fetch you out as soon as they are back on board ship.'

'Thank ye, sir,' one offered to Nicholas. Both were visibly shaking, but they backed away and melted into the forest.

'We have to return to town.' Malachi slapped Nicholas on his shoulder and then stepped down the path to lead the way through the overgrowth. 'I need to be visible, and you need to go and keep going. That brute saw you clear as day.'

'Thank you. You could have kept going with them and deserted me to my fate. The pressgang would not have bothered the village again if you'd left me there,' Nicholas said. 'They would have taken me as a fair swap for their lost bounty — that's if my head had not been cloven in two. No questions would have been asked of them, or my pleas heeded.'

'A living sacrifice, eh? No, I don't think so. Malachi gave his word to you; he asked for the help of a 'friend', and I don't desert mine. Would you?'

Nicholas shook his head.

'No, I thought not. Now, you get back and see to that young lad of yours. I'll ask about town to find out if anyone knows about your two shadows; but I would suggest you move on, sir, quickly.'

'I have business to see to, Malachi.' He rubbed his jaw, satisfied that it was not bruised, and focused on each step he took as they increased their speed.

'Aye, that may be true, but right now you need to be back in the inn, safe and accounted for. Don't do to be found out here, just in case they come a-looking — or, God forbid, they have other groups hitting on more villages or farms. But if I know anything, there'll be a ship waiting for their return, and it will have to leave when the tide's right. They don't often come more than a couple of miles inland around these parts. Tide and time wait for no man. So for now, I reckon they'll be busy enough looking out as to how to fix their boat, bailing it out and trying to get back to yonder ship in time. So let's get back to town.' Malachi walked on.

'Did you ask Dr Sands to send for the parish constable, Malachi?' Nicholas asked after some moments had passed by.

'Aye, I sent word that he should be called; but if the man lived and was in such a state, perhaps seeing to him took his attention from it. Besides, why do you think that Battle is always found in the Rabbit and Hare?' He chuckled. 'He spends half his life in a drunken stupor.'

* * *

Guy went up to the room with a full belly and a more settled heart, knowing that he was safe again, and that the wench would keep him from harm and warn him if danger was near. He walked along the short corridor carefully, for the door to their room was slightly ajar. Guy pushed it ever so gently and listened as it swung wide.

There was no movement or noise from within. He looked and could see that Mr Penn's bag had been upturned on the bed, the contents strewn all over the floor. They had pulled his coat off the door hook too. There was a fob watch discarded by the pillow, clear for all to see, yet it had not been taken. Guy looked at it. It had writing on it — a name, perhaps, but it was not for him to know what, as he had never learnt his letters.

Then Guy remembered the velvet purse. He rifled through the pockets of the coat, but it had gone. His heart sank. He was supposed to have been here. He was supposed to watch over Mr Penn's things — and now this! He did not even know if Mr Penn was in trouble. He had trusted the butcher, but Guy remembered being thrown down a dark hole where the stench had been overpowering, and the rats . . . He shuddered. He would forget it soon enough. When Mr Penn returned, he would find this mess and the pouch gone! It had meant a lot to the crushed man, and to Nicholas, yet his disobedience had let it be taken. If only he had stayed put, he could have fought them off. Then he remembered being thrown into the hole, and a wave of cold fear hit him. He had never felt so small, lost and insignificant in his relatively short life. Not since Ma had died and left him alone, anyway.

He picked up Mr Penn's watch and placed it safely into his pocket. Then he had an idea: maybe Mabel would have seen who came up here. He had failed as a keeper, but he would find out who did it.

He ran back down the stairs, slowing before leaving the seclusion of the stairwell. He peeped around and, seeing no one was looking his way, slunk behind the counter. He waited for Mabel to turn around and find that he had returned to the small barrel seat. She looked a little surprised to see him sitting there, quiet as a mouse, behind her again.

'My, you is a sneaky one and no mistaking,' she said, after swearing when she was startled by his presence.

'Ma'am, did you see who went up to our room whilst we were out?' Another thought crossed his mind. What if it had been her? She might have decided Guy was for the pressgang, and Nicholas was already gone. Who would know who had done it? Why not rifle through their belongings? But then, why leave a good timepiece and just take the pouch? No, the two bruisers must have got to it. They knew what they were looking for — or someone else did.

'No one has been asking for your Mr

Penn. The pressgang sent a man up there, but he weren't in the room long enough to kick open doors and see if there were any eligibles hiding.'

'You sure?' Guy asked, frustration nibbling at him like the rats he had imagined attacking him in the dark.

'Wait.' She smiled, revealing her browned teeth. 'Well, there was only a man who was looking to rent a room. He was interested in taking the one next but two to yours.' She tilted her head to the side; her mass of oily sandy hair nearly fell out from under her old mob cap. 'He was up there a few minutes on his own, as the press were down here and I had to pop back and make sure they weren't helping themselves to me ale or porter. Or me special hid under the counter.' She winked.

'Was he baldy-like?' Guy asked.

'Aye, sturdy-built man wearing a tweed-like jacket.'

'Is he still up there in his room?' Guy asked anxiously.

'Nah, he popped back out; said he'd bring his friend and settle up when he returned. I told him I'd not hold it unless he paid in advance, but he said as he would take his chance. Why, what's amiss?'

'I think he ransacked Mr Penn's things.' Guy watched her mouth set in a tight line. She slammed down a tankard that she had been filling, pulled out a cooper's broadaxe from under the serving hatch, and heaved herself up the stairs at a speed that belied her size.

Guy followed her. She had the broadaxe gripped firmly in one hand. Mabel flung open the door to the room she had been going to let out, but it had not been disturbed. There was no sign of anyone determining to return. Then she went to Nicholas's room and stared at the mess. She swore. 'Bloody hell! I run a respectable house. Did they take aught?'

'I don't know what he keeps in his bag.' Guy skirted the truth. He did not want to tell her about the pouch, for that was for Nicholas to do. He also realised that the only thing of value that he knew that Nicholas had left there, other than the pouch, was an expensive-looking watch, which was now in his own pocket. He swallowed. If Mr Penn did not return soon, he could not prove he had not done this himself to pinch the timepiece. He swallowed again, realising another cold hole might well be opened up for him in a gaol. People were sent to the hulks or to foreign lands for less — or hanged, even. His thoughts made him feel cold inside.

Mabel slammed the door shut. Guy jumped. She waved the broadaxe in his direction. He paled. Without, apparently, realising what she was doing, she continued to speak. 'You stay put behind that counter until we see Malachi and your man return. Then they'll know what to do. Your friend has brought a jinx on us all! Since he appeared in town, all hell has broken loose. You don't dare disobey me, boy!' She stormed off back to her place in the inn. Guy obediently followed, his hand clasping the timepiece in his pocket as if it could send a message direct to Mr Penn — another silent plea for help.

7

Nicholas strode into the inn. He was anxious to make sure that Guy was safe, and to find some much-needed answers to his questions. As he entered, heads turned to face him. Malachi had gone straight to his friends to arrange the food and supplies for the lads, and for men to watch the ship and make sure the sailors left on it.

'Mabel, where is Guy?' Nick nodded his greeting as he approached the counter.

'Did you get them back?' she asked.

'They are safe and in hiding. Guy?'

'He's here.' She poured him a best French brandy from a bottle she kept hidden under her counter. 'Have that on the house with our thanks before you leave.'

He glanced around and watched as the same faces who had scowled at him hours earlier now lifted their tankards to him in a form of silent thanks. He downed the drink in one, which offered his dry throat some pleasant comfort; but as he replaced the glass on the counter he saw the fear on Guy's face as the boy stood. Nicholas had not been deaf to the request for him to leave by the woman, despite her apparent show of gratitude.

'What is it?' Nicholas asked him.

Guy ran around to him. 'Them men have been to your room. They been looking through your things, Mr Penn.'

Nicholas turned and raced up the stairs. He glanced at everything that was on the floor and checked the bag. Mabel arrived as he went through his coat pockets and looked at Guy. He had been about to speak of the pouch when the woman appeared in the doorway.

'Did they take much?' she asked.

'Not a lot,' he replied. 'I had my money on me, fortunately. How did they get past you, Mabel?' He looked at her question-ingly, not accusingly — but hadn't she bragged that she saw everyone and everything that went by her?

'I showed one man up to the room

along there. Apologies, sir; I did not know him, and how was I to know he had followed Guy here? The pressgang, the bloody sailors, were here at the same time. I cannot be in two places at once. I left him to look at the room and make up his mind. Only for a few moments, that's all.' She looked at Guy and then shook her head. 'We had such a quiet town before you arrived.' She stared at the lad, as if pressing her hidden meaning upon him; but when she saw Nicholas glaring at her, she half-smiled.

Nicholas raised an eyebrow, not sure what the implication was, but guessing ignorance and superstition were at its root. 'I'll settle for the use of the room for a little while longer, just one more night, and then we will pay our dues and be on our way.' His clothes were wet; he needed to change.

'No extra charge. Just be gone in the morning.'

Nicholas did not argue. Instead, he folded his spare shirt and trousers, and she made her way back down the stairs. 'Shut the door, Guy,' he said.

'Mr Penn, I . . . ' the lad began to say, but as Nicholas turned and sat upon the bed, dropping the folded clothes to the side and picking up his bag, Guy swallowed and paused.

'You disobeyed me — again! I told you to stay put. I told you to obey me, Guy! This world is not a safe place. You obviously need to learn obedience; and, by God, be made to sit still and learn about it in a way you have never had chance to do before. You were nearly caught by the pressgang. You could have been caught by those men, whoever they are.'

Guy had the good grace to look somewhat shamefaced at the correct accusations, but then lifted his chin up and declared, 'They took the pouch, Mr Penn. But I'd never told Mabel or no one that it was there. I'd have made a stand against them if I'd been here!' Guy stood up, fists balled at his side.

Nicholas looked at him. Guy would have stood and fallen, he did not doubt that. The pouch was nothing; the key, which it had hidden, he had on him in his waistcoat — a wise act, as it had turned out. However, the loss of his timepiece he would grieve deeply. It had been a gift from his father. Their relationship was difficult at the best of times, but he regretted that he had left it in the room. That gift could not be replaced. The timepiece had monetary value, but the inscription was one of the few things he treasured in his life. Everything else was transient — people, places and possessions.

'They would have snapped you in two, Guy. You have yet to become a man. No, you need to be in an environment where you can grow safely. Ultimately, that adventurous spirit of yours can be unleashed upon an unsuspecting world, when perhaps you will be able to deal with the dangers around you.

'Sir.' Guy swallowed and stepped forward. He removed his cap, and from inside of it, he took out the watch. When he had been downstairs, he decided that it would be better if it was not found in his pocket. The timepiece filled up most of his palm. 'I kept this for you. I wasn't stealing it!'

Nicholas's eyes widened. For a moment he was sure that they would give away how much that simple gesture and discovery meant to him. He reached out and took it, then placed it safely where it belonged in his waistcoat pocket next to his heart. A fanciful notion, but one that gave him the first peace he had felt since arriving. Mabel was quite correct — this place had not brought any comfort or luck for him. The plain truth of it was the market town had brought him nothing but anguish.

'Thank you. I owe you for that.' Nicholas stood and collected his things neatly together. Discreetly, he felt inside the bag and made sure that the bottom of it was still fastened securely. It did not pay for the boy to know everything about him or his things.

'Sir, what do the words say on it?' Guy asked, squashing his hat upon his bouncy hair with pride.

'*Victori spolia*,' Nicholas said — at least, part of the inscription did. He saw Guy scrunch up his face, not understanding. '"To the victor, the spoils',' Nicholas explained. 'It is a family motto of sorts.'

Nicholas changed into his dry things and, with feet that were comfortable again, got ready to go. 'Now, you do as you are told. I have a man to find.'

Guy looked up and grinned. Nicholas was taken by surprise at his sudden lift in spirits. 'I know something for sure,' the boy announced.

'What is that?' Nicholas asked as he slipped his greatcoat on.

'If you want to know who those men are, I'd ask your Dr Sands. They were on the river that runs behind his house.'

'Coincidence,' Nicholas said.

Guy shook his head. 'No, sir. You remember when we were helping the man in the butcher's?' Nicholas nodded. 'Well, he said he was going to tell Dr Sands and have him tell the parish constable, but no constable turned up. Then them men are seen out back of the doctor's house. Strange, eh?' Guy looked at him, wide-eyed. 'Why did he want to brush you off and get rid of me snooping out back?' He folded his arms.

'You are accusing the doctor of being involved in some form of subterfuge?'

Nicholas looked at the lad. Guy's brain was always very busy figuring, observing and deducing. Was his imagination getting the better of him, Nicholas wondered, or was there some truth in his observation?

Guy nodded.

'You could be correct, or you could be seeing connections where there are none, like me, which is why I have sent word to someone I know who will visit The Haven for us.' Nicholas picked up his bag and reorganised his belongings.

'Can I stay with you, Mr Penn?'

'For now, Guy . . . just for now.'

8

Amelia Pendleton greeted her father in her usual warm manner as he returned from his early-morning ride. She was as beautiful as always, and possessed a seemingly endless enthusiasm for life. Wilson could not fail to acknowledge that despite her mother's removal from their life, his daughter had blossomed. Amelia was like a flower who had not had the benefit of being allowed exposure to the full warmth of the sun. She was now ready for the picking, but who would make her a worthy husband? There was no one good enough for her, he knew, but at some point soon she would have to be found a match. That 'someone' would have to be a man whom he could control; someone who would obey him through fear or respect. Either way, his Amelia would stay near to him. Wilson needed her innocence; she saw good in him, and he liked that. She was a balm to the soul that Nicholas, it seemed, had often doubted even existed.

'Good morning, my dear.' Wilson smiled at her genuinely; he responded to her with a strange feeling of warmth within his cold interior, she being one of a very select group of people who could conjure up that unfamiliar emotion within him. Then he noticed she was holding an opened letter in her lace-gloved hand. 'Now, my dear, what precious gem do you grasp so tightly?' He saw excitement in her eyes.

'They have come to me from Nicholas.' She opened her letter, and he saw that inside was a folded note for him. 'He wrote to me to say that he cannot join us as soon as he had planned, and asks if I could content myself by shopping a while longer in York before we return to Mayfair. Oh, Father, I love this place. Do we have to return to London so soon?' Her face was filled with hope. 'We must await Nicholas's return. After all this time apart, I couldn't abide coming out for the Season without him sharing in my good fortune; besides, he has had such an unfortunate time because of Mother's dislike of him.' She paused and quickly changed tone when Wilson's expression altered at the mention of his wife Elizabeth's behaviour toward Nicholas. It had been dealt with. 'Mother always claimed that London was so dirty and that we are in better health for living up here.'

He took the note from her, which had been addressed formerly to 'Colonel W. Pendleton', and realised from the use of his old rank, the one that should have rightfully been his but was denied him, that all was not well. His son, distant though he was to him in many ways, knew that when Wilson was needed he would respond, just as Nicholas had been there for him when he was wrongly imprisoned the previous year. It was an experience he hoped never to repeat. Blood, it seemed — even bad blood — still held some strength of a bond within it.

Wilson opened the note as Amelia continued talking about how Nicholas had told her that he looked forward to seeing her again, and hearing about all her newfound friends. *Intriguing*, he thought: not the girl's chatter, but the summons within. He smiled at his daughter, who was awaiting his agreement. 'Very well, Amelia. You shall stay here a few more days or weeks, possibly, whilst I finish off some business with Nicholas. We will have to find something for you to do. You will need a chaperone, though . . . '

'An invitation was sent to me by the Billingtons yesterday. Miss Lydia and Miss Janice Billington are both very good company, and they have recently received the latest issues of *La Belle Assemblée*. Oh, Father, they have asked me to come and share their collection with them! They really liked me when we met at the assembly rooms last month. Please say I may go! Then I will know what everyone is wearing.' She looked as though she would burst with despair or joy, depending on which way his decision went. Fortunately, he was in a fine mood at the thought of a new adventure opening up before him, so was happy that his daughter had her own amusement and distraction provided for.

'Well in that case, I will arrange for Whitaker to be your chaperone, and she can see to your luggage. Grantham will have the carriage waiting for you at the hour of two; and you, my dear, will be made ready to leave punctually.'

She rushed to him and hugged him tightly. 'You are a wonderful father!' Her outburst took him a little by surprise, but he accepted it with his usual understated confidence. 'And London . . . ' she added as she pulled away.

'Amelia, enjoy your visit. Let us take one step at a time. For now, it appears that York has enough to offer us.' He smiled and she stepped back, recovering her polite posture.

'As you wish, Father.' She hesitated, and the smile fell slightly from her face.

'What is it, child?' Somewhere deep inside him he acknowledged that the term was no longer applicable to the beautiful young woman who stood before him. He could not bear the thought of her losing that charm and becoming world-weary like so many wenches he had known.

'What do I say if they ask where my mother is?' She flushed, and her hands seemed to find each other in a nervous gesture of unity.

'You simply hold that pretty chin of yours up high, look at them through those beautiful eyes, smile, and say that she is in poor health — her nerves require that she takes both rest and the purification of the waters. Do not be drawn into which ones — they may presume Harrogate, Buxton or Bath, it makes no matter. Cast your eyes down and look as if the topic upsets you deeply, and then they will change the subject and try to restore your happy heart. There is no shame in having a sickly mother, Amelia. No one need ever know her murderous guilt. She is safely kept away from where she can do people any more harm, including Nicholas. You and I know her mind was confused and needed peace away from all other earthly distractions. They may assume that her situation is one that has affected her physically, and that when the balance of her humours is restored, then she may well return. Just remark that you are hopeful for her swift recovery. They know nothing of her involvement in the events that happened last year. No one does. The murderer killed himself in a final act of cowardice, and with him the truth of the affair died also. Enough lives were lost. Hers is now safe and protected, as is your and my reputations.'

Amelia nodded. 'She will not return to us, though, will she? For what she did was — '

'Amelia, send in Whitaker and I will give her instructions. You set your mind to your visit to see your new friends, and be happy that no scandal will attach itself to you. Enjoy devouring the latest fashions as illustrated in *La Belle*. Unlike your mother, I will allow you the freedom to enjoy yourself in such a fashion, where she would not have. Be grateful for that.' He patted her gently on her shoulder, as if soothing a child — which to him she still was.

She smiled. 'Yes, Father. You are quite correct, as always. Mother would expect me to continue in a respectable way with such people. I will not let you or her down.' She left him, looking totally content in her world.

His daughter's happy countenance was easily restored to her, Wilson thought. He took the note to his study. The message was simple.

Meet me at The Flagon Inn tomorrow at noon on the moor road. Travel light, but be prepared for action.
Yours
N. Penn

Wilson raised his eyebrows. His bastard son still chose to travel under his alias even though the Pendleton name had been given to him. That aside, whatever was afoot intrigued this bored soldier. There was a tap on the door.

'Enter,' he said, and Mrs Whitaker walked in. 'Good. Whitaker, you are to go on a visit with Miss Amelia. You will act as chaperone to her, and you will be expected to remain with her until I return. Her well-being is in your hands, and I expect you to make sure her behaviour is above reproach. You do not leave her unattended, and must make sure that she is never led into a situation that could compromise her reputation. You will leave instructions here with Cook as to what should happen in your absence. I will also be away for some time.'

The woman nodded. He knew that her loyalty was complete. People who owed you their life tended to be more faithful, he had discovered, than casual employees. Content in the knowledge that Amelia would be happy and safe, he called his man. He would soon be riding off into the unknown, just as he liked it, and Nicholas had called him. A balance and a debt would be restored, and he would ride again with the son he loved. Shame, Wilson thought, that Nicholas despised him so much. Never one to dwell on such things, he made ready his bag and rode off.

* * *

Amelia was so excited she had broken her fast early, and eagerly watched her father leave their home from the long window on the first-floor landing overlooking the drive. He always carried himself with such bearing that he must surely look grander than Wellesley himself.

She was going to the Billingtons' estate! Mother would never have allowed her to go off with just a servant. Father was so much more trusting. He was too busy playing soldiers to bother with her. Although she felt sorry for her poor mama, the freedom that she was now experiencing was so much more entertaining than her life had been before. Her warring parents had resulted in her living with the daily bitterness of her mother's troubled mind. But her father had returned and set her free. She breathed deeply, smiling at the pleasure her new life afforded her.

She held her invitation to her breast. It had arrived two days earlier, and she had been awaiting a time to mention it to her father. Along with the formal invitation was a letter from Miss Janice Billington. Amelia had not shown him the contents because it spoke of Janice's brother, Mr

Bartholomew Billington, who was to arrive in some days' time to stay for the next few months. He was an artist, writer, poet and scholar, and Amelia had met him once at the assembly in York. It had only been just the once; she had had a dance with him, followed later by a short conversation conducted discreetly behind a column, but their eyes had met and their hearts had sung to each other. Like birds in the treetops, they had called to each other, he had said; and now she was to visit with his family, staying under the same roof as him. It was too much happiness for her heart to contain.

As Wilson Pendleton rode out of sight, Amelia rested upon the window seat, watched him disappear, and closed her eyes as she remembered the feeling of dancing with Bartholomew, her admirer — and, she believed, her soulmate; for why else would her emotions be stirred so? He was tall, fair, and had travelled — unlike Wilson and Nicholas on dirty battlefields, always fighting, so their sense of romance had been lost to adventure. No, Bartholomew had visited places of learning and wisdom. He had drawn and painted great lakes and mountains. He had breathed in life, he said; and she desired to share in that experience, breathing alongside him.

With her mother away and her father off on his business, there was no one to stop her living and loving the man whom fate had placed in her path. She smiled; *Amelia Billington* had a warm, rounded sound to it that made her being swell with pride and possibilities. She supposed she would have to find out where the family's wealth came from. She hoped it was not purely from trade. She did not really know how her father would view totally new money, but surely an artist was someone to treasure and encourage. Besides, her happiness was paramount to him. She could see that. Those hard eyes of his softened as soon as she greeted him.

Content in her thoughts, Amelia decided there was nothing in the world now that would prevent her from future happiness. Once the wars ended, she could envisage going on a honeymoon with her Bartholomew that would take in Paris, Rome,

Athens, and many more great cities. They would see the home of every artist, philosopher and poet that they could think of. Her father would be so pleased whilst he was occupied doing things with Nicholas. They had to look to the future, and hers had never been so clear or accessible.

Amelia sighed as she imagined her life with Bartholomew. Then a tap on the door interrupted her bliss. 'What is it?' she snapped.

Mrs Whitaker approached. 'Miss, I have packed our things, but would like to check that there is nothing you particularly want with you that I may have omitted.'

Amelia looked at the dour woman. She was to be chaperoned, the only aspect of the arrangement that she had forgotten. Her freedom would have to be planned carefully. Surely, though, she could outwit such a miserable creature as stood before her. Her father had poor taste in servants, she decided.

'Very well,' she answered, and walked past her. Everybody had a weakness or something they wanted. All she had to do was discover what Whitaker's was, and then she could still have her freedom. She smiled to herself. Freedom would be hers — and so, in time, would be the handsome and charming Mr Bartholomew Billington.

9

Nicholas found the parish constable in the old inn, The Rabbit and Hare, at the opposite side of the town. He approached Mr Battle, but Guy stayed by the doorway with Nicholas's bag clasped firmly in his hand. The man was drinking with one leg up on the settle's seat; he looked extremely comfortable.

'Mr Battle?' Nicholas stood at the end of the table.

'Who wants him?' Bleary eyes looked up in Nicholas's general direction.

'I wondered if you could tell me if an accident was reported to you yesterday concerning the mowing down of a stranger in the street.' Nicholas had sat down opposite and leaned forward so that he could talk without the few people who were there listening to their conversation.

Battle slipped his boot onto the floor, and Nicholas sat back whilst the man regained his composure and managed to prop himself upright. He pushed down with his hands on the table top. Battle's head tilted backwards with an unnatural force in order for him to appear at all sober. It was clear to Nicholas that the man was incapable of standing. 'I repeat my question, sir. Who is it . . . who wants to know what I have been told?' He slammed the palm of his hand down on the table; the gesture did nothing to Nicholas, but Battle cringed at the noise it made. A few heads turned their way, but none gave him much attention. Nicholas shook his head. This man was responsible for keeping the law and overseeing fair play. The magistrate depended on him to bring issues before him, yet he looked incapable of even looking after himself.

'It is an easy enough question to answer. I am a visitor to your town who wants to know if a man died yesterday as a result of an accident I witnessed on the street.' Nicholas watched the man's face. He was taking in the words, but Nicholas wondered if their meaning was lost to his dimmed senses.

'You are heartily mistaken, my man!'

Nicholas wondered if the man's vehemence was purely to force his mind into forming words, or if he was trying to cover up something.

'The only accident that happened hereabouts was a simple slip of foot, and the good doctor — Dr Sands, that is — is seeing to the poor fellow's needs. There was no reason to involve myself or the magistrate.' He smiled and added, with a gust of stinking breath, 'Good day, sir.' He took a swig of his drink, seemingly contented that he had despatched Nicholas's curiosity successfully.

'So the man lives still?' Nicholas persisted.

'Of course he does, or why would he need a doctor's care? Are you simple, sir?' he spluttered.

'You are certain?' Nicholas ignored the man's insult, as he wanted him to slip up. The words uttered were as if he had dragged up a pre-learnt reply through a drunken mist.

'On my mother's life, sir. Now go before you vex me further.'

Nicholas thought about reacting to his insolence by slamming the man's face firmly into the table before him, but decided he had better not risk a night in the lock-up. Instead, he walked off.

Battle shouted after him, 'Who did you say you were? I demand to know!'

Nicholas walked past Guy in disgust, making no reply. He stopped long enough outside the inn to take a look around. There was no sign of the two bruisers who had arrived at the butcher's. 'There is no more to be done here,' he said.

'Mabel thinks we brought some sort of jinx here.' Guy sniffed.

'Do you believe in such nonsense, Guy?'

'No, they bring it upon themselves because they hide from the truth.' He looked up at Nicholas.

'What do you see as the truth, then?' Nicholas paused long enough to hear his ward's words.

'A man was killed, the body searched and stolen, and his death covered up.'

Nicholas looked at his young, wise friend. 'You sound certain.' He took his bag from the boy.

'So is you, sir,' Guy added. 'Or why would you not accept it and just walk away, leaving that key in Dr Sands's keeping?'

'You think so?'

'If not, you would not be asking your questions,' Guy remarked, and followed Nicholas as he walked off down the street.

'We shall say goodbye to Malachi and be on our way.' Nicholas did not look down at the boy. It unnerved him, the way he read people and saw things. Yet he admired him also. He had a gift that needed nurturing, but Nicholas did not know if he was the one to take on such a task. In Wilson's hands, he could be turned and used; he wanted Guy's heart to stay healthy and true. His plan to leave him with Amelia was waning again.

'Where to, Mr Penn?' Guy asked, but Nicholas just kept walking.

'Don't you know?'

He entered the front of the butcher's shop, where Malachi had been busy serving a woman. She turned, smiled nervously at Nicholas, and left rather quickly.

Malachi shrugged. 'Don't worry about her; she is skittish by nature. People seem ill at ease ever since the storm and the accident.' He wiped his hands on a rag. 'Come through the back.' He nodded to the room where his carcases were hung.

'You heard anything more of them?' Nicholas asked. He tried to hide his repulsion at the smell of death that filled the room.

'Yes.' Malachi looked at his visitor. 'I have heard that your two men have been seen here twice before — once following the hapless young man who graced my slab when he went to meet his love some time ago; and once on his return, chasing him down the street and into the road.' He shrugged.

'So who are they?'

'That, we do not know. However, the lass who just left here thinks one was ill, because she saw him visit the good doctor before she left.' He looked at Guy. 'After seeing them take off after the lad, thinking the pressgang had got him, one of them went to Dr Sands's office. She had baked Sands a cake and had just left — or so she says. Who's to know why a wench sees a doctor?' Malachi half-grinned but did not add further comment.

'Dr Sands? I thought you respected him.'

Nicholas saw the man laugh. 'Oh, I respect all kinds of folk. That don't mean that they are all saints. You know, in my experience, people are not all bad or all good. There are shades in between. What shades he has, I don't wish to know, unless he threatens me or mine.' Malachi looked thoughtfully at Nicholas. 'He did me a good turn. I owe him for it, but that don't mean I'm his or any man's puppet. But I know where to draw my line.'

'Thank you for your help, Malachi.' Nicholas took a step toward the door. 'I hope you can stick to your line.'

'You are leaving town without finding any answers?' Malachi asked casually.

'I think there are some puzzles we are not meant to fathom. Good day.' Nicholas had no desire to involve the man further. Whatever had happened to the young stranger, whatever the importance of the key and whatever the connection between them and Dr Sands, Nicholas had decided that Guy would be kept away from it, as would his new friend Malachi. The man had saved him from being caught or cleavered. He had a business and family and needed to be there for them. But Sands and Malachi clearly had some shared history.

★   ★   ★

'So where are we going?' Guy asked as they walked into the stables.

'You are going to stay with a young lady I know called Miss Amelia; you met her fleetingly. I am going to spend a little time with my father.' It seemed strange acknowledging the man by his rightful title. So many times he had furiously sworn to break away from his shadow and not look back; yet now, in the wisdom of calm hindsight, he could see that not all the mistakes made could be laid at Wilson's door. He was only human after all — or so it seemed.

'You are going after those men, aren't you? You and the colonel! There's something more than fishy about them. I'm sure one is a sailor,' Guy added.

'Why should you think that?' Nicholas asked as he tightened the saddle on his horse.

'He had one of them knives,' Guy said as he placed the bag safely behind the saddle and fastened it well.

'One of what knives?' Nicholas wondered what Guy had seen now.

'Them with the carved bone handles. They're scumshores . . .'

'Scrimshaw, a pattern etched into bone.' Nicholas looked at the lad.

'That's it. He had one tucked in his belt. I saw it when he shook me. So he was either a sailor, or he had taken it off one,' Guy reasoned.

'Or he had bought it off one, or been given one by a friend,' Nicholas offered.

'Types like him don't buy things, they steal them; and who would be *his* friend in the way that they'd give gifts?' He shrugged. 'Not surprising, then, that he was able to set the pressgang on me whilst the other one rifled through your things. Old friends, no doubt. Good distraction, though. Those sort of friends do things for each other — you know, thick as thieves,' Guy explained, as if Nicholas had no more knowledge of life than a sheltered maid.

'You may well be right, but why they should be connected to a respected doctor of Sands's standing is a bigger puzzle.'

'That's simple. He don't get himself dirty, does he? Don't go to visit normal folk and their ills. So he pays the roughs to do his dirties for him. He only puts himself out for them that have money.'

Nicholas smiled and mounted the horse, letting Guy put his foot in the stirrup, pulling him up behind him. 'It's time we brought a bit of hell to a certain haven.'

10

Amelia was greeted with such a welcome that she felt as though her arrival had been anxiously awaited.

'Come, Amelia, you must meet Mama; she has arranged for tea to be served in the green room. The garden looks beautiful from there.'

Both Janice and Lydia eagerly escorted Amelia into the house. Once inside, the formal introductions over, Amelia enjoyed polite conversation whilst Mrs Whitaker was shown to their room and then to the servants' hall, where a tray had been placed for her. 'I must stay with Miss Amelia — I am her chaperone!' she protested, and refused to sit down.

'You will eat where Mrs Billington decides is fit.' The tall woman who had escorted her to the room turned and left without a further word.

Mrs Whitaker was not convinced. She made to hurry to the door, bumping into another serving wench as she left the room. 'Mercy, woman! You could have been scalded!' The woman — short, and friendlier in manner than the officious lady who had brought her down the stone corridor — was holding a bowl of soup cradled in a clean cloth in her outstretched hands. It smelt very appetising.

'I must apologise, but I am a chaperone to Miss Amelia Pendleton, and I must stay with her,' Mrs Whitaker hurriedly explained.

'They won't thank you for interrupting their chatter, now, will they? Why not sit yourself down, knowing the young miss is safely with Mrs Billington and her girls for a while? Have yourself some good food, and then I'll take you back to her.' The woman raised a brow and smiled at her.

'Very well, I suppose that will be acceptable — just whilst I eat and she makes her introductions. But from now on, I must insist that I accompany her whenever Mrs Billington is not present.' Mrs Whitaker sat down at the set place, and with silver spoon lifted she eagerly ate the excellent food provided upon fine china plates. This was the most pleasant treat she had had in a long time, and was not to be passed over. So, contentedly, she enjoyed her food.

'That's it. You tuck in, and when you are done I will send for Mrs Blackman, the lady who showed you in here, and then you can insist all you like to her.'

The woman left. Mrs Whitaker was given the finest food; she had rarely felt so full. After the soup, a platter of freshly cut ham and game was brought to her; and even a glass of wine was provided, alongside a sweet jelly with fresh cream that smelt slightly of brandy. She could only presume this was the leftover fare from the previous night's dinner. Once she had finished, Mrs Blackman arrived as promised.

'You may unpack your mistress's belongings, and then you may join her and the ladies on the terrace.' The woman stood aside so that Mrs Whitaker could leave the room with her. 'I am the housekeeper. If you need anything, you should come to me.'

'Thank you, Mrs Blackman, I will. I am Miss Amelia's chaperone, and as such I will expect to be with her.' Mrs Whitaker was waiting for her to advise her never to 'insist' on anything, as the woman's manner was very confident.

'Of course. We would expect nothing else,' she said, and continued to take her up a servants' staircase to the upper landing. 'Your rooms are here.' They crossed the richly coloured carpet to the bedchamber directly opposite. 'Pull this bell cord when you have finished unpacking, and I will take you to your lady.'

Mrs Whitaker was left in the sumptuous room, which was delightfully light, the walls covered in hand-painted Chinese wallpaper with beautiful peonies and small birds making a magical scene and adding colour. The four-poster bed in the centre of the wall contrasted with its heavy tapestry hangings in a rich red accentuating the warm colours of the carpeting. A room off to the right provided the bathing facilities; another cupboard room to the left with painted plain walls, a cot bed and washstand, was obviously for her, the servant.

Mrs Whitaker felt the quality of the linen sheets upon this humble bed and wondered at the filling of the mattress, as it was soft. She felt so full; the wine had made her feel sleepy. She knew she should unpack her mistress's clothes and return to her side as Mr Pendleton had ordered her to do, but she just thought she would try the bed out for a moment or two. She pulled off her boots, put her bonnet on the small window shelf, and lay down. This was bliss. Happy and content in her moment, she fell fast asleep.

* * *

Amelia was delighted with her greeting. Soon Mrs Billington was called away, so the girls all sat on the terrace and enjoyed fresh lemonade and chatted; but then a rather severe-looking servant arrived whom they called Mrs Blackman, and they too had to excuse themselves for a few moments, leaving Amelia quite alone. She stared across the lawn to the lake and the folly and sighed. This was lovely.

'Miss Pendleton, forgive me if I break

your peace. What a pleasant surprise this is!'

Amelia stood up and turned around to see him, there before her. She knew she was being awkward and that her cheeks had no doubt coloured slightly. 'Mr Billington. What a pleasant surprise.'

He stepped forward, leaving less than an arm's gap between them; she could smell his cologne. 'I hope I did not shock you?'

'No; I was admiring the view, Mr Billington,' she said, and gestured to the lake. As if on cue, a peacock strutted across the lawn.

'How bad it is that my family should desert you so. Perhaps you would care to take a walk with me, and I will show you my favourite fountain.'

'That would be very pleasant,' Amelia said without a moment's hesitation, and fell into step with him as they strolled away from the terrace, along a path that took them into the hedged garden to the secluded fountain beyond.

* * *

Wilson arrived at the Flagon Inn, but there was no sign of Nicholas or the boy. He bought himself a drink and sat in the chair by the bay window, which gave him an excellent view along the moor road. He waited patiently for a few hours before he saw his son riding along the road toward him; the young lad seemed to be with him still. Wilson found it ironic that Nicholas should have taken on an urchin. He'd learn soon enough that they either stole from the one who helped them, or in gratitude Nicholas would find out that he would have a devoted follower for life. Perhaps he had learnt something from his father's ways after all.

★　★　★

Nicholas dismounted; he stabled the horse, noticing the fine animal already there. Wilson had arrived. They entered from the back of the inn. He paused long enough to order a simple meal for Guy. Once the plate was paid for, he gestured toward the empty stool by the fireplace. 'You sit by the warmth of the fire and

105

keep your eyes open.'

From his perch, Guy would be able to watch both of them as they talked and yet be able to see who came and went through the doorway, whilst quenching his thirst on ale and sating his appetite on a slice of beef and a cold potato.

'He has a better life than a dog,' Wilson noted as Nicholas sat down opposite him.

'So he should have. Thank you for coming. Have you eaten?' Nicholas asked.

'Possibly, you are welcome, and no.'

'Let's try their brandy. They'll have some French, no doubt. The mutton smells freshly cooked.'

Nicholas went back over to the man, who was keeping himself busy fixing a shelf behind the counter. He ordered their food and returned to a seat away from the window, gesturing Wilson to follow him.

'You intrigue me, Nick. What is all this about?' Wilson sat down, glancing around as if to indicate that there was hardly anyone else present.

Nicholas waited for him to settle down and pay him full attention, and then pulled the small key from his waistcoat and showed it to his father. 'It is all about a man who died, I believe, in very painful circumstances. Though I am to understand that he is recuperating in a soldiers' hospital called The Haven.'

Wilson turned the key over in his hand, studied it, and then gave it back to Nicholas to replace safely in his pocket. 'Speak, man. You have my attention.'

Nicholas gave his version of events as Wilson listened with great interest. 'He must have thought he would be able to retrieve it from you once the men had finished with him or give up the chase.' Wilson shook his head. 'You say he was dead.'

'Both the butcher and I believed he had not survived.' Nicholas folded his hands on the table. 'I want you to make innocent enquiries at The Haven as a man with rank. See what you make of the place. Visit it as if you are interested in placing a friend, colleague or relative within it. Meanwhile, I will visit the man's father on his estate and see if I can determine if he thinks his son still lives. I hope to seek out who this 'Amelia' is that the key was meant for. It cannot be our Amelia, surely.'

'Why not wait for me, and we can go and visit them together?' Wilson said. He seemed quiet and subdued.

'Possibly, but first I would take Guy to stay with our Amelia,' Nicholas said, and saw Wilson look up at him in surprise. 'I won't involve her, but will ask if she has heard of the Root family. Just in case . . . '

'Why would she need the boy around her? If I wanted her to have a pet, I would buy her a puppy.' Wilson glanced at Guy. 'You still do not know how loyal he is. You trust too easily, Nick. He has not been tested.'

'He did well in finding out some information last time.'

Wilson refused to comment. The previous affair of the young women's murders only brought him memories of his wife's betrayal.

'He needs to learn his letters and have some education. It would be cruel to throw him into a school. He has been used to roaming, has no family background, and would be the butt of cruel jokes. He would fight back and spend his life in punishment. However, Amelia could busy herself teaching him the basics, and then perhaps I might pay for a tutor. See if that mind of his can be sharpened further. He has some intelligence, Father. I would like to see it used wisely.' Nicholas looked at Wilson, expecting him to agree or come up with the viewpoint that he should not be trusted with his daughter, or to insist that the discipline of an establishment would do him good.

'Too bad, Nicholas, for Amelia has gone to stay with her new friends, the Billingtons. They have rented a place on the outskirts of York. They are moneyed. I understand that much of it came from lands in this area: wool, alum and copper. The elder Billington died of his excesses, but his wife and daughters live well enough. There is a son who visits occasionally, but he is a complete wastrel, spends his time admiring things, and doing nothing. He will make some wench a poor husband as he can never keep to one alone. He flits and floats whilst others die in battle to protect his precious existence. The girls seem pleasant enough, though. They have been bred well like Amelia, they know what is expected of them, and Mrs Billington is really quite a catch.' Wilson smiled slowly.

'You are already married, sir,' Nicholas said quietly, and saw a flash of what could have been anger or hurt in his father's eyes.

'I hardly need reminding of that!' Wilson snapped in return, and then lowered his voice. 'She can see a deserted man's plight at being abandoned in my prime by my weak-minded wife.'

Nicholas shook his head. The words spoken were not in jest or sarcasm, but as a true statement. Nicholas knew that his father was a man who was immeasurably comfortable within his own skin. 'That is your concern, sir. Will you help me with my enquiries or not?' he asked.

'Of course I will. I am here, am I not? I liked it when you called me 'Father'. However, I suppose for our next journey together that 'sir' might be a better compromise. After all, you do not travel with your God-given name, one that was given to you at great personal sacrifice by me.'

Nicholas did not rise to the taunt. Wilson's rift with his wife had been caused by his meanderings and had finally been made worse by his acceptance of Nicholas, his bastard, as his heir. His own mother had died through Wilson's short-sightedness, so Nicholas was hardly going to feel guilty that the man had finally acknowledged his own offspring. If his wife had been able to give Wilson a son, Nicholas doubted he would have been acknowledged. He glanced at Guy as he sat like a medieval spit boy by the open fire, and decided that most likely it would have been his place if Wilson had legitimate sons.

Seeing that Nicholas was not going to reply or respond to his comments, Wilson continued, 'The boy cannot go to Billington's, so he must stay with you or here sweeping out the floors and fetching barrels.' He raised an eyebrow, but when Nicholas shook his head, Wilson sighed and continued, 'Or we could find somewhere for homeless waifs and leave him there. They teach them their letters there, do they not?' There was a cruel half-smile on his lips.

Nicholas shook his head. 'Out of the question; he stays with me. Once Amelia returns, then I will speak to her of Guy's future. For now we have a mystery to solve and a man to find.'

Wilson stood up. 'I will change into my old uniform and then find out what is happening at this Haven place. They are not to know that I am no longer in any active service.'

Once Wilson had taken his bag and left, Guy came over to Nicholas. 'He doesn't like me, does he, Mr Penn?'

Nicholas patted the lad's shoulder. 'Don't take it personally, Guy. He doesn't like anyone much.'

'I think he does.'

Nicholas glanced at him and waited for him to explain what his comment meant. 'You think he likes himself only.'

'No, Mr Penn. I don't think he does, but he respects you,' the lad added.

'Come,' Nicholas said, and led the way outside, shaking his head.

11

The two men rode off together, Guy holding onto Nicholas's jacket tightly as he sat behind him. There were few words exchanged between the riders until they reached a copse of trees on the northern edge of the woodland that shielded the town from the low-lying loop of the river. Behind this was the place called The Haven.

Nicholas pointed into the trees behind them. 'There is a track that cuts through the woodland; it skirts the ruins of an old abbey. I will wait there. If you do not return in a few hours, I shall come and see why not.' It had been the hiding place of the two young men who had escaped from the pressgang with Nicholas's help. They would be back home by now.

'Very well.' Wilson moved the horse forwards. 'This man, the patient, you say he had fair to ginger hair and many broken bones.' Wilson glanced at Nicholas with a wry smile upon his face.

'Yes,' Nicholas replied.

'Then he shall be easy to seek out. Why not leave the boy on watch for my return?' Wilson rode off, obviously not caring what they decided to do. He had a mission to accomplish; and that, Nicholas realised, was what the man needed most of all: some danger to lose himself in. He was wasted behind a desk or frittering away his time in clubs. Now they were set again on another mystery. It appeared there was purpose to their lives once more.

'You want me to watch for him, Mr Penn?' Guy asked.

'We both will.' He let the boy down and dismounted. 'We'll tether the horse in the abbey ruins, and then find a good vantage point.'

* * *

Wilson rode up to the iron gates. The building was an early Georgian mansion, built of ashlar stone in a baroque style. What looked like an oak tree was carved into plaques in the wall at either side of the entrance. They were ornate, with branches pointing upward upon a strong trunk and roots spread out below. However, the black wooden sign that had been fastened to the gate itself was bold in its copper-coloured writing: 'The Haven: where the sick of limb or mind can find respite or a caring cure after so bravely serving their country'. Wilson doubted how 'caring' it was, as he had seen the poorest form of human suffering in such places as asylums, confinements and gaols. The latter he had personally experienced only too recently, so that he actually felt a cold shiver run along his spine as he recalled being trapped in the narrow cell, kicked by the scum that had arrested him. Thank God, if there was one, for Nick, loyal to the core. Being confined had unnerved him, and Wilson did not allow that to happen. Emotions were for the weak.

He opened the catch holding the gates closed, pushed it wide, then rode up to the building itself. No one appeared to greet him and take the horse, so he dismounted, leaving its rein tethered to a boot scrape by the steps of the grey building.

The windows, he noted, were quite large, but had shutters closed within, which seemed to defeat the object of letting light into the building. He tried the door, but it was locked, so instead he pulled on the large knocker and waited patiently.

After some moments the door was opened by a woman dressed in a grey uniform, which somehow matched the building. Her apron was clean, as was the white hat. In fact, it looked pristine to him, as if she had not 'nursed' anyone. Wilson noted the bunch of keys that hung from her belt, reminding him of a gaoler.

Seeing his smart appearance and fine thoroughbred, the woman smiled at him. 'May I help you, sir?'

He made no effort to sound personable, but held his normal authoritative manner; she was a servant and he was used to ordering them around. 'I would like to see whoever is in charge.' He held out his card, walked in front of her, and entered the building.

The interior was subdued. It was dark, and the furniture sparse to the point of being hardly existent. One table had been placed in the large entrance hall just to the side of the door; the rest of the chequered flooring was empty. There were marks on the walls where paintings had once hung. To the right was a wall of stone, which had no markings upon it, that obviously had once been covered with a tapestry; an iron hanging rail still remained, but the place had the feeling of a home that had been gutted. It looked bare, cold and neglected. He could smell despair. If this house was to become a true haven, it was going to require a lot of work, not to mention fresh air and an investment in some decent furnishings, he thought.

'Dr Sands doesn't like folk visiting here unannounced, sir.' The woman was now standing inside the hallway, but her hand held the large door open as if inviting him to leave. 'Can you tell me what it is that you want, and I'll tell him you called?' She looked down at the card and then up at his face, swallowed and added, 'Sir.'

Wilson stood before her, the noise of

his boot heels echoing around the bare walls as he walked over to her. She opened the door even wider and stepped aside, but he ignored her gesture and faced her down, peering into her eyes. He stood an inch over six feet. He bent slightly towards her, intimidating and challenging. His stance had the desired effect as he saw her eyes dart from side to side, avoiding his directness. Her hand let go of the door and she grasped her palms together in front of her as if her arms were creating a barrier between them.

'You expect me to tell you the details of my affairs?' His voice raised slightly at the inferred incredulity of the request.

'No . . . no . . . of course not, sir. I meant that Dr Sands is in his town office at present, and well, there is no one person in charge here at this exact moment. Therefore, if you leave me a message and where he may make contact with you, I can make sure that he receives it and a more convenient time can be arranged for you to see him — in person, that is.' She took a discreet intake of breath.

'This is a home for injured soldiers, is it

not?' Wilson snapped.

'Yes, sir,' she answered, seemingly surprised by his insinuation that it was not.

'Very well — send word to him that he has someone here seeking a place of recuperation for a brave but fallen soldier. Meanwhile, I will look around and see if the place is suitable.' He walked forward.

'Send someone?' she repeated.

'Yes!' His voice was now raised, as he was sure there was no one there who would challenge him.

'Very well. You should wait in here, sir, whilst I find a girl to deliver your message.' She pointed to an office that had ample light within it. 'But perhaps if you left your card and address where you can be contacted — '

'I am not leaving when I have made time to travel all this way! Tell them to hurry; I have not got all day.' Wilson stared at her.

'Please wait in here, sir.' She closed the door to the office after her and left him in the room.

He smiled. Fool, he thought. The desk was large and, as he expected, locked. The cabinet, which should have held papers, was almost empty — just a few letters of request for rooms or treatment. The desk, made of polished mahogany, had nothing other than a pen and inkwell stand upon it. He took out a lock-pick from his pocket and had it open in moments.

There was nothing of import, but he felt around for a secret compartment. His fingers triggered a clasp that revealed a false bottom. Lifting this up, he reviewed the papers within. Bankers' drafts, a promissory note from a local gentleman, another and another. 'He owns people's debts!' Wilson whispered, realising that in so doing he basically was buying the people: a magistrate, another doctor, an innkeeper, a list of ladies' names that had sums next to them — all married. Interesting. This man was buying up the debts of the town. With the women, he was buying what? Most would be small debts by his standards, but they would have the same effect upon the debtor — they gave the man power and control over the community.

Wilson left the papers as he had found

them, carefully replacing the false bottom, and then locked the desk as if it had never been tampered with. The bookcase to his left had a few medical books upon its shelves, but again was half-empty. It was as if the place had not yet opened properly or was in the process of closing. Either way, this was no hospital where people were recovering. It had the smell of a much more lurid business — the business of controlling or blackmailing people and influencing their destinies.

He looked around the room. On top of the bookcase was a simple model barrel; next to it was a small bronze figure of a cooper raising his hammer. Wilson saw the shutters at the windows, which were closed and clasped firmly shut; he opened the door slightly and peered out. There was no sign of a soul about. He presumed the wench had taken the message herself.

He went up the stairs two at a time and walked the length of the top landing. As he pushed doors open, empty rooms or empty beds greeted him. Where were the nurses? Where were the recuperating soldiers? The place was as silent as the grave.

He quickly made his way back downstairs to the ground-floor wing. Here there were a few injured men lying stock-still in their beds, but even they seemed to be too still. Seeing a man propped up in a chair with a strap seemingly holding him upright, Wilson walked in and looked around him, but the room only had a bed, the man, and a chair and a small table. Again, it was obvious that paintings and furnishings had been removed, as their ghostly outlines were plain to see on the faded walls and from the change of colour on the floor.

'Soldier?' he said, but the man did not respond to him.

Wilson took hold of his head, holding it upright and looking at the man's eyes, which were heavily lidded. He raised one of the lids with his finger. He was clearly drugged. The patients in the other rooms all seemed to have been subdued in the same way, with no sign of anyone looking after them. Under the blankets the other men were strapped onto their beds; with their senses dulled they could not go anywhere.

Wilson made his way to a room at the

furthest end of the corridor. The door was locked. He knocked, not expecting to hear any movement from inside. His hand found the lock pick. It was a gift from a man who owed him his life in a battle when Wilson was his captain. He had the man show him the tricks of his old trade from when he had grown up in the infamous Seven Dials of London. It had filled in part of his education that had been missing from his more academic Oxbridge teachings.

Before he lifted the pick from his pocket, the handle of the door turned slowly, and a small-framed wench opened it and looked up at him. Her pale face showed fear as she saw this strange man standing before her. He reached over, pushing the door open wide. She shrank back and froze. He ignored her for a moment and strode inside. Her eyes looked at the open doorway behind him as he walked over to yet another bedridden figure. She moved further back with each step he took towards her.

'Don't run from me, girl,' he ordered. 'You do not need to fear me if you answer my questions and do not lie.' He pointed a finger at her and peered into her eyes as if he had some mesmeric power. How easy it was, he thought, to control a weak or fearful mind.

She gasped. Clearly, running had been her first thought. It was obvious to him, but the girl's wide eyes told him that she thought he could read her mind.

This room, unlike the others, was airy. The blinds were open. He turned and looked at the young wench. In the daylight he could see that she was a pretty little thing, quite comely, though not, he thought, quick of wit. Her uniform looked as if she had been tending her patient well. Her sleeves were turned back. There was a bowl of soiled water still warm at the side of the bed.

The figure lying within it was, by the little that was visible of his face, a man who was about Nicholas's age, with fair to ginger hair. His eyes were puffed, his jaw was supported by a bandage, and his lip looked cracked. Wilson lifted the covers and saw the body bandaged, one leg lost below the knee. He did not smell rank; instead there was a strong odour that he could not place, but it suggested herbs or flowers. The man appeared to be being treated by means of some sort of poultice upon his limb beneath the compressed strapping. He was thin of frame and quite pale.

'What is this man's name?'

'I . . . I . . . '

'How long has he been like this?' he asked her.

'I . . . I . . . '

'Answer me!' he shouted at her, and she jumped back.

Her hand shot to her mouth but she answered, 'A few days, sir. He is badly, badly ill, sir. Please be quiet. He must not move.' She ran to the bed and replaced the blankets so that the man was tucked in like a babe.

'What is his name?'

She shook her head. 'You should speak to the doctor, sir. He don't like people bursting in here. This is a place of healing, and he said it should be quiet.'

With one hand, Wilson took hold of her arm and spun her around. She screamed.

'Sh!' he reminded her. 'This is a place of quiet. What is his name?'

'Mr Root, sir. His name is Root.'

Wilson leant over to him. 'Mr Root?' he whispered softly into his ear. 'Can you hear me?'

'He can't talk, sir.'

'Sh!' Wilson snapped a finger at her. She backed away. He slipped his hand under the blanket and found the man's. 'Can you hear me, Root?'

He was not sure whether the man's finger had flinched or moved deliberately. There was a noise behind him and he glanced around. Damn — the girl had run off, he presumed to get help.

'Do you remember the key?'

Nothing.

'The key for Amelia?'

Flinch.

'Does the doctor know of it? One flinch for 'yes' or two for 'no'.'

Flinch . . . pause . . . flinch.

'Do you wish him to have it?'

Flinch . . . pause . . . flinch.

'Do you know who has it? Who you gave it to?'

Flinch.

'You do?'

Flinch . . . flinch . . . flinch . . .

Wilson stood instantly. He had no wish for anyone to understand that communication had taken place. There was no possibility of moving the man. He turned around to see the woman who had allowed him into the office standing in the doorway. Her cheeks were flushed; she had obviously been hurrying. The younger nurse was standing behind her with a small bottle in her hands.

'Dr Sands is out at present and cannot be contacted. You must go now. We cannot have people roaming around here at will. Dr Sands insists that only complete peace and rest will mend the patients. It is time for his medication. Please leave; we don't want them to be disturbed.'

'You intend to make me?' Wilson asked, as he turned to face them.

'No, she don't, but I do,' a man's voice sounded out from behind them. The figure came into view. He was large of frame, balding, and held a pistol in his hand.

'I merely sought to find out for myself

how well the sick are tended here before making arrangements with Dr Sands.' Wilson stepped away from the bed and watched the young wench run over to the patient, spoon and elixir ready. The man would be kept out of his senses like the other inmates, he was sure of that. 'Good day,' he said, and walked in front of the man with the gun. As he did, the fellow backed away so that he could keep Wilson in his sights. Wilson paused. 'Who do I have the pleasure of the hospitality, sir?'

The man stared at him and gestured with the pistol that he should keep going.

'Very well,' Wilson said, and noticed as he turned that whoever he was, he had a seaman's taste in knives, as one with an elaborate carved handle adorned his belt.

Wilson strolled back out into the bright autumnal sunshine, glad to feel it upon his face. The smell of fresh air replaced that of gloom and despair.

He looked back. The brute still stood on the stairs, pointing his pistol at him. The audacity of the man, Wilson thought, and marked the man's card in his mind. He smiled, touched his hat's brim with the forefinger of his right hand, and smiled before mounting his horse. They would meet again, but for now he had at least something of worth to report back to his son. He smiled at the notion of him reporting to Nicholas. How quickly the world could change, he mused as he rode back out.

12

Nicholas listened with interest. 'Then he definitely lives. The poor sod. I thought he was dead. I could not feel his pulse, and his body was so bruised and broken. Even the butcher, Malachi, thought he was gone.' He hated the idea that he had abandoned a man who could have been saved.

'Well you are not a physician, Nick. You are a soldier. You have seen so much death that perhaps you have come to expect it when a man is so ill, but away from the battlefield the odds of survival improve — or they should. The butcher, you say — Mr Malachi Gunnings, by any chance?' Wilson asked as they stood waiting in the shelter of the abbey ruins. It had not been that many months ago since Wilson had escaped from the gaol and hidden in such a place, waiting for his brave Amelia to bring him a fresh horse. How innocent she was, and how reliable Nicholas had been.

Nicholas looked to Guy. 'He intro-duced himself as just 'Malachi'.'

Guy nodded. 'Mind, he did leave after declaring the man was as good as dead to go give word to Dr Sands, didn't he?'

Wilson looked at Nicholas, adding, 'Well there cannot be two butchers with the same Christian name in such a small place. Dr Sands holds a debt that was outstanding on the lease of the shop for five pounds and six shillings. He holds notes on a number of local businesses and, it appears, some of the wives of the town. He has people go to him in his office rather than doing rounds. However, he seems to eat well at the local houses and also have regular visits to his more affluent patients, even by their own carriages. Your doctor, this man Sands, seems to acquire the debts of his patients; so he is either a man with a lot of capital and an extremely kind heart, or a very shrewd businessman who is empire-building. Either way, he is more than your average village doctor.'

Nicholas listened intently to Wilson's

recount of the man Root's brief exchange with Wilson; that was, if the 'flinches' were more than just twitches. 'We go to his home, then, and see what his father has been told of this. I understand from Dr Sands that Thomas Henry Root is his only heir, so he should be indeed grateful to the good doctor for saving his son's life.' Nicholas shook his head as he picked up his horse's reins.

'What is it, Nick?'

'You say he knew who he had given the key to?'

'He responded to my question, though whether that meant he knew who you were or he would recognise you again if he saw you, I know not. We were interrupted. He is kept sedated. I doubt I could break in and ascertain more. They will have given him an opiate to dull his pain and senses if they think anyone is trying to question him.'

Nicholas placed his foot in his stirrup, and then leant down to pull Guy up behind him. 'Then we go straight to Middleham and hope that the mystery can be unlocked from there.' Guy chuckled at the quip but Wilson did not.

Wilson had hold of his reins and had been about to take a firm grip of his saddle when he froze mid-action. 'What did you say?'

'I said we should go and see his father,' Nicholas explained as he sat aright with Guy happily holding onto him, no doubt ready to continue their adventure somewhere new.

'You said we were to go to Middleham!' Wilson's tone had changed.

'Yes, his father owns an estate there.'

Wilson swung onto his horse. 'Does he indeed! We'd better make tracks then. Perhaps you can tell me any other details that you have omitted from this mission before you forget them whilst we are on our way.' He kicked the horse on, and it slipped slightly as it made its way through the narrow muddy track.

'So what is at Middleham that he don't like, Mr Penn?' Guy asked.

Nicholas thought for a moment. 'I'm not sure.' But he mused something or someone was. He knew from Wilson's abrupt change of mood that he would have to wait for the fire in the man to dampen down somewhat before pursuing the question. There was, however, nothing more that Nicholas could tell him. They rode for two hours in silence before reaching a coaching inn on the crossroads from where they would leave the moor road and head across country to Middleham.

Upon arrival at the inn, Wilson dismounted, almost throwing the horse's reins at the stable lad. 'See he is fed, watered and rested, boy, and brush him down!' He tossed the boy a coin and stormed inside the cruck-built building. Seeing the innkeeper, he shouted, 'Ale,' demanding a jug of his best as he made his way to a quiet corner where he could sit by the open fire. Nicholas saw him toss his hat onto the settle next to him and lean back, his eyes staring at the fire's flames.

'Two plates of stew, and bread,' Nicholas ordered from the innkeeper, and paid for two more drinks of ale. He deliberately smiled, as the man was obviously perplexed by Wilson's manner.

'Don't I get to eat, sir?' Guy asked discreetly.

'The food is for us. He'll have taken care of himself. Now be quiet and sit in the corner. Don't interrupt us, and avert your eyes.' Nicholas ruffled the lad's hair. He was always thinking of food.

Guy nodded and slipped along the settle into the corner, avoiding staring directly at Wilson. He happily slumped into the seat and waited with the men in silence until their food arrived.

Wilson had not ordered, but when the plates arrived he took Guy's and told Nicholas to order another if he wanted the waif to eat. Nicholas did, pushing his own plate to the boy as he wanted to talk first now Wilson had broken his silence. Guy did not have to be asked to tuck in. His attention seemed to be completely on the food.

'Are you going to explain, Father?' Nicholas spoke quietly. He saw Guy look up in response to the warm tone within his words.

'Explain what?' Wilson snapped back.

'Why the dramatic reaction to the

mention of Middleham? Why suddenly your old angry self has returned to us. I thought we left him the day we solved the murders of the poor young women around Gorebeck.'

'I was driven out of the army!' Wilson barked, and then stared at Guy, who immediately looked down.

'One day that wrong will be righted, Father . . . one day, I promise. But for now, what is it that grieves you so? What is it you hide from me? I am your son, am I not?' Nicholas knew he was using sentiment with a man who rarely showed any. Wilson desperately wanted Nicholas's respect, and possibly even his love.

'Don't try playing with me, boy! You use that word when you mean it with all your heart. You still have one, so do not toy with one who has lost his. It is a very unwise thing to do,' Wilson said quietly as the third plate was brought to the table.

The wench looked at Wilson and gave him a smile, winked at him in a way that was very inviting, and swayed her hips as she turned, glancing flirtatiously back at him. He gave no response and so, discouraged, she sloped off.

'Harlot! So many of them!' Wilson glared at the food as if it had offended him in some way.

'What is it?' Nicholas persisted. 'Tell me. Do you know the Roots of old?'

'That is where she is, Nick.' Wilson breathed deeply and recomposed himself, sitting upright and poking his food with his spoon.

Nicholas looked at the serving wench and then at Wilson, who shook his head at him. 'Not that flighty bitch. The other one — my darling wife. She is housed in Middleham. I placed her there with a nurse, a keeper, and left her the means for her to have a doctor call on her each month to make sure her needs are being met, that there is no cruelty of a physical nature taking part. Her mind was to be fed with books, painting and music. If she slipped further into madness, then the asylum awaited her; if she rebelled and showed herself completely sane but driven by hatred, then she would answer for her crimes. Her companion was to be a woman of middle years who seemed to have an even countenance after losing her home when her brother married. She would have a home so long as she acted as Elizabeth's keeper and stayed within the grounds of the hall. They were not to fraternise with other local people, and her identity was to be kept simply as Miss Elizabeth, spinster of fragile mind who needed rest and peace. If these rules are broken, she knows that in no uncertain terms her next place of rest would be more confining.'

'So?' Nicholas asked blankly.

'You do not think this at all odd?' Wilson stared at Nicholas. 'Am I never to be free of this woman's interminable shadow?'

'The place we seek may be far away from hers. The Root family may have no connection to us. Amelia is quite a common name.' Nicholas sighed. 'I agree there does seem to be an amazing coincidence to all of this, but one that makes no sense. Until we find something that does, we have to keep our minds open. We will have to stay here tonight.'

Wilson nodded and added, 'Well we'll

keep our minds and eyes open, but we'd better make certain of this; for if she is connected with that feeble piece of humanity that lays broken and abed, incarcerated in his own pain and prison, then I want to know what it is that connects them. Why would he pass a key to you? Why would he mouth the name of your lovely sister in your ear? And why, when I swore I would never return to the place called Middleham, am I sat here in an inn on its boundaries set to do exactly that? You tell me that, Nicholas — why?' He slammed his fist down on the table with such force that ale spilled from the jug and the spoons jumped on the wood.

Guy shrank back as far into the corner as he could, but his small voice offered one word: 'Fate!'

Wilson looked at the boy, as did Nicholas, and both men smiled then laughed. 'Out of the mouths of babes!' said Wilson, and he took a long drink before staring at Nicholas and repeating his question: 'Why, then?'

'Perhaps because this time it is I who need you?' Nicholas looked into the man's impenetrable eyes and saw that he was genuinely beginning to smile.

He raised his tankard to Nicholas and said simply, 'Now that I will drink to.'

13

The Root family manor was located in lands at the furthest end of the town. Middleham consisted of a single line of houses and shops stretched out along the banks of the river. The road continued beyond this small settlement to cross the Pennines linking the northeast of the country with the northwest. Mrs Elizabeth Pendleton now existed in a house built in grey stone amongst woodlands on the outskirts of the town screened from travellers' views who crossed the narrow part of this country admiring its vast open spaces. Hers, however, were now extremely limited.

'Do you wish to find Root's manor, or are we paying her a call on our way?' Nicholas queried.

Wilson hesitated. He stared at Nicholas; for once the man appeared indecisive. 'We . . . ' He looked around him and then calmly announced, 'We find the manor, we 'root' out the truth of this family and their connection with the man in the bed, and then perhaps I might visit her. You may accompany me if you wish, Nick, but he — ' Wilson pointed his gloved hand at Guy without turning his attention to him. ' — has no place in this. He stays with the horses and out of sight. Otherwise, he can choose to wander and go his own way. His ears have heard too much already.'

'Very well,' Nicholas agreed. 'To 'Root' Manor then,' he said, and once again saw Wilson's mood change.

*   *   *

The gates of the manor were indeed impressive as they approached. The drive the other side of them obscured the view of the house, but the ornate design of the iron was quite striking and unusual. Nicholas admired the distinctive pattern, which seemed to be a craftsman's interpretation of a tree worked within the framework of the two gates. The roots spread out below the trunk as wide as the branches did above it. The points of both flicked upwards. Where the two gates met in the middle was the central trunk. Nicholas thought it ingenious. He let the boy down so he could open one, allowing the men to ride inside. They waited until he was back with Nicholas, but Wilson was staring at the gates.

'I have seen that design before,' he said.

'Where?' Nicholas asked.

'Carved into the walls at each side of the gates of The Haven. I didn't connect the spread of the roots with any significance or representation, thinking it just a grand oak fancifully designed.'

Nicholas rode alongside his father. 'That would infer that the property that Dr Sands now inhabits belonged to this estate — or still does.'

Wilson nodded.

'Perhaps he won it — you know, as one of them debts you said he acquired?' Guy said.

'Who?' Wilson asked. 'Root?'

'No, the doctor. Isn't that more likely?' Guy added.

'We waste time,' Wilson remarked. 'I told you that boy is a party to too much information for his young ears.' He rode on until they both could see an old Jacobean house, ornate and unusual in design, so unlike the geometric style of newer buildings that were the fashion now, though it seemed to fit its surroundings far better, Nicholas thought.

'Interesting,' Wilson muttered. 'Very interesting!' He dismounted.

'You stay with the horses, Guy, and please remember to keep quiet. You can always voice your thoughts to me, but I would advise you to keep out of his way,' Nicholas warned him. Guy nodded.

Nicholas walked up to the red-brick building. The contrast of the rectangular blue-black diamond-shaped tiles was quite dramatic. A liveried servant opened the door to them.

'Good day. Is the master of the house at home?' Nicholas asked and smiled politely. Wilson stood looking around them, his eyes taking in as much information as he could. Nicholas knew this, even though his demeanour gave the impression of someone who was simply lost in their own thoughts.

'He is,' the man answered. His hair was

greying and his uniform had seen better days, as Nicholas suspected he had.

'Inform your master that Captain Penn wishes to speak to him,' Nicholas said.

The servant looked a little thrown. 'Come in, sirs, and wait a moment whilst I see the young master.' He stepped back and let them enter the dark and wooded entrance hall. Nicholas and Wilson exchanged glances at the mention of the young master being there.

The servant gestured to an ornately carved hall seat placed against the wall. 'Make yourselves comfortable, sirs. I won't be long,' he said, and smiled before starting his way up the stairs opposite the door.

'I wonder if he has been here since the place was first built,' Wilson said dryly.

Nicholas smiled. The tapestries that adorned the stairwell looked in need of a good dusting and mending. The place did not appear as though money had been lavished on it for some considerable while.

'It feels as though we have stepped back in time,' Nicholas commented, and stood up to look at the oak-panelled wall opposite and the family portraits that adorned it. The square-panelled ceiling above contrasted effectively with the wood but was in need of a good clean. The portraits were modest, as they were of heads and shoulders and not the person in full. Therefore, the money was either tightly controlled, or this part of the landed gentry had not been affluent for the last century. He noted that the walls were hung with expensive full-length portraits of earlier generations, possibly the founders of the building.

Meanwhile, Wilson was also looking around and through door jambs. He found a library-cum-office on the opposite side. It had a similar mahogany desk in it as the one that he had found within The Haven. The same style bookcase was standing against the wall next to the window. Atop it was the cooper's figure ready to strike the barrel. These pieces were identical to the ones he had found in the sparsely furnished office of the other building. So his son lay in a bed in a house that had been in the Root family, even if now its ownership was suspect.

They heard the shuffling of the servant's feet as he made his way to the top of the carved oak staircase. He stopped, holding on firmly, seemingly a little out of breath. 'The young sir will see you both, sirs. If you would care to come up.' He half-smiled as if in a silent plea not to make him go down to them to lead the way back up.

'Very good,' Nicholas said, and strode up the stairs two at a time to follow the man down the corridor to a bedchamber to the right. The carpet, he noted, was threadbare in parts. This was no rich man's home.

Nicholas prepared himself to see a fragile old man abed, thinking how ironic it would be if both father and heir were in the same precarious situation of hovering between this life and the next. Instead, he was surprised to see that a man no older than Wilson was standing with his back to a large bay window, before him an easel and in his hand a brush and palette. The man was busy painting.

'Good day, sirs,' he said brightly.

Wilson and Nicholas entered and looked around to see the subject of his work laid across a chaise longue in a diaphanous empire-line dress with nothing much underneath it to disguise her natural curves. Her mass of fair hair was piled high in curls on her head with tendrils allowed to flow down at the side of her neck, falling across her young bosom. She blushed as the strange men entered, and Wilson hesitated, seemingly taking a moment to admire her form.

'Beautiful, my dear.' The artist placed his brush in a wide-necked glass bottle and began to wipe his hands on an old cloth. 'You may change and go about your normal duties. We will continue at the same time tomorrow. Now run along and see that dress is hung properly!' He looked at the two men. 'I do so admire the work of Francois Gerard. His portrait of Madame Recamier is a masterpiece of seduction. Do you not think so? Still, no peeping, now.' He wagged a finger at Wilson, whose attention was elsewhere. 'Tell me, sirs, what brings you to our neck of the woods?'

He removed his painting shirt and pulled on a new one. 'Gerard, see to it that this is clean for tomorrow. I cannot abide working through grime.' He tossed the soiled garment at the manservant, who nodded, picking it up from the floor as his reactions were too slow to catch it. He bowed and made his way back to the door. 'Go tell Sally to bring in some maids of honour, tea and seedcakes. I do so love a sweet treat.' He smiled. 'Go on, man; she won't bite. You've seen breasts before, haven't you?' He glanced up at the ceiling, and the man entered the side room where the serving wench was changing. Gerard was heard apologising as he entered.

'Mr Root?' Nicholas asked, questioning whom they were actually addressing. He was confused, as this man had dark hair; and although he may have just been old enough to have fathered Thomas Henry, he did not seem to fit with his surroundings or in a fatherly mould.

His question was met with brevity. 'Good lord, man — no, I am not Mr Root!'

Wilson, who had been watching what the maid was doing in the side room, and making no apology for looking on from his vantage point near the doorway, spoke out. 'We came to see the owner of this house: Mr Root. So who, pray, are you, sir, if you are not he?'

The man's smile dropped and he looked at Wilson directly. 'Why, sir, I am Mr Digby Belasis, a guest here of my dear family's friend Mr Nathanial Root, owner of this splendid hall, who is also my patron.'

'Belasis!' Nicholas heard Wilson snap back the word under his breath, and instantly spoke out to distract the man's attention away from his father's surprised expression. 'I apologise for disturbing you at your work, but we appear to be in the wrong man's room. Now, if you'll have the servant show us to Mr Root's quarters, then I am sure we can be about our business and away from yours.' He turned toward the door, tapping Wilson's arm to get his attention, for he had somehow frozen in time, staring at the artist.

'No, sir, I am afraid that you cannot do

150

that, as he will not wake from his afternoon rest for at least another hour. So please do join me; the tray will not be long, I am sure. Old Gerard may be slow of foot and wit, but Sally has plenty of energy and fine young legs to hurry our repast to us. I should know.' He winked at Nicholas. 'I have studied their forms regularly.'

Nicholas did not respond. He found the man repulsive, but was determined to be civil. They had to talk alone with the senior Root.

'Please call me Digby. Are you men of the arts? We could amuse ourselves with recounts of our tours.' He smiled hopefully, looking at Nicholas. Wilson's face had that cold, detached mask that Nicholas could read so well. Staying in the room with this man would be dangerous. For whatever reason, Wilson had taken an acute dislike to him.

Nicholas nodded to Digby. 'Very well. However, our recent 'tours' have been somewhat limited . . . '

'To the bloody carnage of battlefields against Napoleon,' Wilson put in, before

151

sitting on a chair near the door.

'Spoken like a true soldier. Well, there are men of arms and men of art. I am, for my failings, one of the latter. I simply would not do to be on a battlefield, although in my mind I could imagine one in fine detail and paint the victorious soldier set against the wretched scene of the defeated fellows for you, if either of you two gentlemen would like to commission a portrait. I can be very flattering with the brush.'

'Indeed,' Wilson said casually. 'I agree, you would not do.'

Nicholas pointed to the canvas and changed the subject quickly. 'May I take a look at your work, Digby?'

The man glanced at Wilson awkwardly but moved protectively toward the canvas. 'Not an unfinished painting, but I could show you some of my finished work. I have some in here.' He stepped forward and offered for them both to enter the side room. On the walls were hung a variety of paintings. Some were celebrating the female form in the style of the classics, with figures dressed in Grecian robes; others were portraits in the Dutch style. The man,

Nicholas thought, had some talent, but his strokes were too bold when they needed subtlety, and his proportions did not totally convince.

Nicholas moved around the room, looking at each in turn and making polite comment. He was relieved when the tray of food arrived. He made himself comfortable on a seat by the window table in one of two leather armchairs. Digby followed him, anxious to know what he thought of his work and if he could commission work from him or recommend him to a friend.

Wilson hung back. He had no appetite. The name 'Belasis' stuck in his throat, like a claw ripping his heart out. For that was what the wench had done. She had been his true love. Elizabeth belonged in a picture — a beauty that could be admired, yet forever trapped where she could do no man any harm; but of course she already had. Him.

He ambled around the small room, showing his open distaste for Digby's style. Wilson looked to the covered canvases not yet mounted in the corner. He flinched at the first attempt at a still life that affronted his finer taste, then at a nude wench. He wondered if Digby understood anything about the sheer beauty or subtlety of a well-proportioned female form; but then, as he flicked from one to the next, that face struck him like a knife penetrating into his chest. She was in front of him as he envisaged, trapped in life, in still life; and so, he realised, would he be, until he was rid of her curse. One word he muttered: 'Elizabeth!'

★ ★ ★

Nicholas wondered what was keeping Wilson. When he saw him leave the room, cool, calm and with a seemingly pleasant smile appearing on his face, he knew his father was dangerously near to losing his temper. Something about Mr Digby Belasis's name, something about the man's work perhaps, had ignited that dangerous spark in Wilson's eyes. Nicholas had seen it happen before a battle or when dealing with the aftermath; but since being sent back to England, it had only happened once, and that was when Wilson had been accused of murdering a wench who turned out to be his own daughter. All of that was well behind them now, so what had he seen or heard that was driving that same cold hatred that Nicholas had learned at cost to read and dread?

14

Amelia was happier than ever she had been. Opportunities for her and her beloved Bartholomew to be together kept arising. He whispered sweet things to her. Flattered her. Spoke of having his friend paint her portrait and seemed on the brink of proposing. He had even stolen a kiss. It was all she could do not to laugh at Whitaker's indignation at being treated like the servant she was. Whatever her father had thought of sending her as a chaperone was beyond Amelia's understanding, although she smiled at her own cunning; she had not given him much time to make alternative arrangements.

It was with some surprise then that she found the woman appearing in the summerhouse, where she had expected to meet with Bartholomew. 'Miss Amelia, there you are. You really should tell me before wandering off. Your reputation could so easily be damaged should you be discovered in such an isolated place with, say, Mr Billington. Then what would your father say?' Mrs Whitaker entered the shade of the stone columns that surrounded the glass doors where Amelia had been waiting patiently.

'I am sure no one would see or mind on his own estate!' Amelia snapped and looked across the lawn, then along the path near the lake to see if he was making his way to her.

'His estate?' Mrs Whitaker queried. 'I am afraid you are misinformed. The Billingtons do not own this land. They are using it for the summer and will return to Northumberland in the autumn. This is merely an opportunity for the younger generation to find suitable spouses or benefactors to allow the family to continue living in such a style. This land belongs to the late Mr Billington's brother, Bartholomew's uncle, who is in his Devon estate at present.'

She moved closer to Amelia, who was listening, quite stunned, by what she was hearing. Bartholomew had certainly led her to believe he was a man of means and that this estate was well within them. 'Have you been gossiping with the servants, Whitaker?'

'No, miss; I have been talking to them and listening. Take care, miss.' Whitaker met Amelia's glare with equal confidence. 'Your reputation and family name need protecting. Your father would expect it.'

'How dare you talk to me so!' Amelia snapped.

'I dare, because someone has to make you see the trap that you walk into before it closes in around you, miss.'

She turned to walk outside into the sunlight. 'I will dismiss you if you ever speak to me like that again! You are my servant!' Amelia, enraged, wanted to stamp her foot, lash out at the woman and knock her all-seeing, all-knowing face into the mud. But Whitaker merely glanced back at her as if looking upon a naughty child.

'You cannot, Miss Amelia, because I am employed by your father, and him I both respect and fear. Please come back to the house. Mr Billington has gone to town.'

Amelia watched the woman walk away.

Tears streamed down her cheeks. She must compose herself. There must be a way for her to escape the suffocating grip everyone had on her life: her mother, the madwoman; her father, when he was there; and now this annoying servant who thought herself too grand for her position as chaperone. Bartholomew may not be rich — he may be too ashamed to admit it — but she loved him for the man he was; and no dried-up, jealous widow-woman was going to remove her one chance of happiness.

She wiped away her tears and breathed deeply. She would ask if she could ride. That would put Whitaker in her place as she could not. Miss Amelia had been taught to by the best — her Nicholas. If only he were there he would give her his blessing to be happy with Bartholomew, her love. By the time Amelia had walked back to the house, she had a plan in mind. She would ask for a horse on which to ride around the grounds, and then she would go to the town by herself and see if she could find Bartholomew. After all, she had ridden out on her own with her father's blessing when he had needed her help, and he was not at all bothered about her reputation then. No one was going to stand in her way of happiness ever again.

★　★　★

Wilson pulled out the painting of Elizabeth from the sideroom as Nicholas made an attempt at polite conversation with Digby. The afternoon was slipping away.

'Oh, you have found a painting you like perhaps?' Digby stood optimistically and looked at Wilson, who tossed it on the bed.

'How did you come to paint this lady?' Wilson asked.

Nicholas saw Elizabeth's face staring out of the canvas. Even on a flat surface, her image made a shiver of unhappy childhood memories run along his spine. He glanced at his father, understanding the man's change of countenance.

'She is my cousin, sir. She sits for me when I visit her for her painting lessons.' He smiled nervously, as if desperately trying to fit together the pieces of a jigsaw. 'You know her?'

Nicholas intervened. 'You visit her?'

'Why, yes. Her husband set her up in Bluebell Cottage at the other end of town. She has painting lessons and encourages young artists. She needs the peace for her nerves; she suffers with them when in the turmoil of society. However, Lizzie is as witty as ever.'

Wilson let out a long sigh.

'Tell me, does Mr Thomas Henry paint also?' Nicholas asked. 'Does he visit her to be encouraged?' He saw the man's face colour slightly and realised that part of the truth was plainly revealed.

'Why, yes, but his father does not wish him to . . . in fact . . .'

The door burst open and a stocky gentleman dressed in a double-breasted burgundy smoking jacket, leaning on a silver-topped cane, appeared. He was pale and had greying hair. 'No, by God, I did not — and I am surprised, Digby, that you would break my trust and cover for him.'

'Mr Root . . . I apologise, he made me . . .' Digby's grovelling made Nicholas's stomach turn.

'Get out! Pack your things and leave! I should never have let him talk me into allowing you and your friends into my home!' He then turned to Nicholas and Wilson, whilst Digby sat down and sobbed, holding his head in his hands. 'Please come with me.' He began to lead them back downstairs.

Nicholas followed, but Wilson hung back a moment. 'Digby, did your cousin give anything to you or Henry to be passed on, perhaps?' He left his question vague.

The man sniffed. 'Why, yes. How did you know?'

'Instinct,' Wilson quipped. He thought Digby was stupid enough to believe he was serious as he remembered Elizabeth receiving a letter from her 'gifted' cousin when in London. He had been told something from a person claiming to have received a message from the afterlife! Damned fool. An artist, and delusional too.

Digby nodded knowingly. 'I understand — I could tell you had . . . depth. Henry told me he had to go to town and find Elizabeth's daughter, not the wretch — pardon my words — of a husband who has left her incarcerated in her solitude. She gave him a small gift for her dearest daughter Amelia with secret instructions as to how it could release her fortune and unlock a future for her — for them. It was to be delivered to Amelia when Dr Sands next visited Henry's father, so that their paths would not cross.'

'Mr Root does not know of this?' Wilson asked, barely able to comprehend how such a gullible fool as Digby could survive at all.

'Absolutely not.' He stepped over to Wilson. 'You see, she never forgave him for taking her childhood home.'

'Then why did she not give the item to you, her cousin, and instead trusted it to Root's son?'

Digby's sobs had disappeared as he became immersed in his narrative. 'Because she wanted the house back in the family and her daughter to be near her again. Henry had met Amelia previously on their trips to Gorebeck on market days, and well, she wanted the two to be wed. He met her last at an assembly room in York. However, he could not get near her because

Amelia's brother had accompanied her and kept her close. So when Henry's father asked why he was going to town, he made up some fancy tale that he was seeing his friend Bartholomew. It was true, as Amelia had been invited to stay by his sisters.

'You see, the Root family won this hall from the Belasises in a gambling debt of my father's, who inherited it when Elizabeth's father died. The Roots had their family emblem replace ours on the gates and the hall renamed. The old man always believed there was hidden treasure — jewels — here, but never found them. The ideas of fools. I mean, if Elizabeth had married, any jewels would have been claimed by her husband.'

He shook his head. 'I thought Nathaniel Root had some sense of guilt or obligation when he let me stay here, but he only wants a share in my earnings and to use me to look inside other properties, finding out which families are in need of money. You must despise me, sir; but I have no home, so I must put on my friends again. Thank God Bartholomew is back for the summer.'

'Bartholomew?' Wilson repeated.

'Bartholomew Billington,' Digby offered. 'I didn't catch your name, sir.' Digby looked at him. 'Have we met before?'

'No matter.' Wilson stepped out with urgency in his stride and caught up with Nicholas shortly after they had entered the library.

★   ★   ★

Mr Root had stormed into the room, not bothering to see who followed him, making directly for a tray that had been placed with a decanter and three cut-crystal glasses upon it on a table by the fire. He walked straight over to it, poured himself a glass, and downed it in one. 'Please help yourselves, gentlemen. I am afraid I am in very low spirits, as this day I have received the most grievous news.'

Nicholas poured them both a small glass of the French brandy, noting its origins; this man either had old vintage or was buying from smugglers, directly or indirectly. 'Grievous news?' he repeated and held out the drink to Wilson, who once

165

again had a determined look to him.

'Yes, my son.' He paused to clear his throat. 'I have received word that he has been struck down by a carriage in the street and has been badly injured. I will ride to see him tomorrow. What have I done to deserve such damnable bad fortune? He is all I have to pass on my estates to, and now . . . '

'Our condolences,' Nicholas offered.

'Why could he have not come back injured from battle with glory shining his way? Instead he has to stumble under a bloody horse, no doubt after drinking with his wastrel friends. Well, now he will have to fight if he is going to survive. The letter said he has facial injuries and has lost his right leg from below the knee. Damn him!' The man poured himself another drink and sank it in one go. 'What business do you have with me?' He looked at them as if he had just realised how much of his personal grief he had revealed to these strangers.

'We were passing and were intrigued by your home. We will leave you in peace,' Wilson said, and stepped backwards.

'Peace? What peace can I have now?' The man walked to the entrance hall.

'Key?' Wilson asked. Nicholas slipped it to him and then distracted Root whilst Wilson lingered a moment, picking up the decanter and pouring one last drink. As soon as the two men were away from the half-open door, he poured the liquid back.

A few minutes later, Wilson returned to them, licking his lips. 'My thanks for your hospitality, and condolences for the situation with your son.'

Without further word, they returned to their horses whilst Root revisited his brandy. Guy was nowhere to be seen.

'Guy!' Nicholas snapped, and the lad's figure dropped from a tree like a windfall.

'Mount up quickly. We go to save my daughter's reputation!' Wilson kicked his horse into a canter whilst Nicholas grabbed the boy and swung him up behind him.

'That man came and went, Mr Penn,' Guy shouted to Nicholas as they rode away.

'Who, Sands?' he shouted back; and Wilson, who was alongside them, looked over to the boy.

'No, that man who shouted out 'Thief'

and tried to have me impressed.'

'Sands is in this up to his neck!' Nicholas snapped.

'We will try to save the hapless son once I have spoken with the witch,' Wilson shouted.

'Too late,' Nicholas replied. 'He is dead. The man who lay in the bed — which leg did he have missing?'

Wilson thought and replied, 'The right one, as he said.'

'Exactly! The man who we saw fall had crushed his left leg. I thought I knew a dead man's pain when I saw it, and that man was not going to survive. Sands has a substitute in the making, with a convenient facial injury. If he can fob off the father long enough, he can keep the funds coming in whilst he treats his patient. But why were they chasing Thomas Henry Root in the first place?'

'They wanted the Belasis treasure that he held the key to,' Wilson replied without further explanation, and kicked his horse on at speed. He only stopped when they had ridden through Middleham. 'Nicholas, Elizabeth hid something from me.'

'What? Her heart?' Nicholas snapped back.

'Treasure.' Wilson smiled. 'All the years we were married, she kept something from me, which was rightly mine. Her maiden name was Belasis, and that excuse for a man is her cousin. Through him she met Thomas Henry Root, an impressionable young man who desired my Amelia and who happened to be the heir to Elizabeth's family home. How the woman plots and plans.'

'Where does Sands come into it?' Nicholas asked.

Wilson answered, 'He picks the bones of the rich and weak. Thomas Henry, like her cousin, like the pariah Bartholomew Billington, fall into debt, wager beyond their means and lose their inheritances. They become puppets to the likes of Sands. He climbs the social ladder and becomes rich along the way. He has crossed the line, though. He covered up a death and sought to steal an inheritance instead of being grateful for what he has gained so far. In the throes of this, my daughter is in the sights of a cad, a liar!

He will not lay a finger on her or else he will see it cut from his body as he draws his last breath.'

'But the man in the bed responded to you. Surely he could not have if he did not know what happened.'

'His fingers flinched. I read into it what I wanted to. If he was a soldier with no care or future, who had been offered a chance to take the place of a fallen son, he would hardly be in a position to refuse. He may or may not know what Sands planned. He could not speak, and without care his leg and life could rot. Besides, they kept him, like the others, drugged beyond sense. Sands has done nothing that can be proven wrong unless we discover what they did with the body of Thomas Henry Root. Once Amelia is safe, somehow we have to find out what he did with him. Then he can face his charges.'

They rode at speed, Nicholas taking the lead even in front of Wilson. The notion that Amelia might be in danger spurred him on. When they finally slowed down, it was Guy who coughed out the word, 'Sirs!'

'What is it, boy?' Wilson snapped.

'The men in the barge — they do his dirty work. Find the man with the scrimshaw knife and you'll find your answer to Mr Root's resting place. He was the one who brought word to the old man, so he must be around somewhere.'

Nicholas grinned at Wilson, who stared pointedly at the boy.

'Obviously,' Wilson replied. 'Nicholas, we need to split up.'

'Agreed. I look for the scrimshaw man and you make sure that Amelia is safe,' Nicholas suggested.

'Very well. Make sure you get him. He pulled a pistol on me in The Haven!'

Both followed the road at speed back to the crossroads.

'I will see her safe and then meet you in the inn,' Wilson said.

'No, at the butcher's — the lad will be waiting there with word. This Malachi knows more than he has shared with us, from what you have told me.' Nicholas checked the key was safely back in his pocket. He had listened to his father's words. 'I will use the key, don't worry. You were, as usual, very observant.'

Wilson grinned. 'I am glad that you acknowledge I have some saving graces. You will need these,' he added, and held out his lock picks from his saddle bag. 'Now go.'

15

Nicholas headed straight for The Haven. He made no explanation to Guy, who clung in silence to the back of his jacket. Once in the trees beyond the building, he sheltered there for a moment and waited for the light to fade before he made his move. Guy had secured the horse and waited patiently at Nicholas's side for his next instruction.

'What are you going to do, sir?' he asked cautiously.

'We are going to break into the man's office and recover something that rightfully belongs to my father. I also intend to set a town free.' He turned his face to the lad, who was staring at him unsure, as if he had not heard him correctly.

'We are going to break in?' he repeated.

'That's right.'

'I'm not a thief,' Guy protested.

'You are committing an act of charity for the man who saved your life, for the one who has helped clothe you, and because I ask it. Satisfied?'

Guy nodded, but looked far from it.

★ ★ ★

Amelia had taken a direct route across the open land to the edge of the avenue of trees that shielded the estate from the road. She was soon out of the drive and making her way toward town. She knew it was a rash act — she did not want to appear wanton or desperate — but she must speak with Bartholomew. For a servant such as Whitaker to dare to say such things to her was beyond tolerable. She would have Bartholomew put the woman in her place and return her back to her father immediately. Then things would be made right with Mrs Billington, who would of course take the word of her son if not Amelia's. Why should her happiness be continued to be marred by lesser people, when she had found someone who truly loved her? His touch made Amelia's whole body sing a lovely tune in her mind. She smiled at the thoughts and memories of his gentle but extremely provocative caress. He had held her hand, cupped her face with his fingers and drawn her to him, kissing her tenderly.

They had been in their favourite place within the fountain garden, hidden from view by hedges on all sides. She had stopped him when his hand had found the top of her stockings. Amelia had not realised that he had so deftly lifted her skirt. The waft of cool air and the movement of his flesh on hers as he had striven to explore further had made her panic and she had stood aright, letting out a girlish scream. He had stepped back, equally shocked; but she apologised, felt childish and awkward, and had run away to return inside. He would obviously have thought she loathed him, when in fact it was the shame and realisation of her desire for him to continue that had caused her reaction. Now she would explain, and then he might even forgive her and propose, for he had acted as only a husband should.

Amelia looked to the track ahead; she

was being careful of the horse's footing, as the recent rain had left the road heavy going and consequently slippery. Despite her doubts about the wisdom of her actions, she continued determinedly.

★   ★   ★

Nicholas and Guy climbed over the wall into the grounds of the home and then skirted the lower floor windows on the side of the building that housed Dr Sands's office. Nicholas finally found one that was unlatched. Lifting it first with his fingers and then with his shoulder, he managed to open it wide enough for Guy to slip inside. Once done, the boy could open it to its full extent and let Nicholas in.

Together, like ghosts, they tiptoed around to the office door. Wilson had given meticulous instructions as to the layout of the building. Nicholas opened the door slowly so he could see the hallway. The light was dusky, as the shutters on most of the ground floor windows were closed. Daylight would soon be going anyway. There was no sign of anyone, so Nicholas led Guy into Sands's office. The lad stayed close, and Nicholas could see how used he was to being invisible and light of foot. He might not have been a thief, but he certainly would make a good one.

Nicholas made straight for the desk. 'Keep watch, boy!' he whispered. He used Wilson's lock pick to open the desk drawer, then released the secret compartment as his father had instructed him and removed the papers. Quickly relocking the drawer, he swiftly lifted a chair up to the cabinet. With the papers in his pocket he climbed up, took the small key out of his waistcoat pocket, and used it to release a catch that caused the end of the small barrel to fall open. He caught it in his fingers before it clanged against the top of the unit, and grabbed the contents. Placing them in his other pocket, Nicholas quickly relocked the small barrel and replaced the chair. All looked as it had been before they arrived. He gestured to Guy that they beat a hasty retreat. Leaving via the office window, they closed it to so that nothing looked disturbed.

It was with great relief that they were reunited with the horse and making their way back to town. Nicholas rode to the back of the inn and tethered his horse there away from prying eyes. They traversed the narrow alleyways behind the main street.

'Guy, go to the back of the doctor's and tell me if there is a barge waiting there. Be careful that no one sees you, and come straight back to me. Do not wander off!'

Guy nodded and darted down an alley opposite. Nicholas continued on his way toward the butcher's shop.

$$\star \quad \star \quad \star$$

Wilson saw a rider in the distance coming from the direction of the Billingtons' estate. He slowed to see who it was, but when he realised it was Amelia he rode to meet her as fast as his horse could safely traverse the ground. Wilson slowed as he approached. 'Amelia!'

Her initial reaction seemed to be one of pleasure, as it always was when he appeared before her; but then it slipped to another look completely — that of surprise or panic. All was not well with her, that was clear to Wilson.

'What is it, Amelia?' He brought his horse alongside hers. She looked anxious, as if she did not know what to say, and his heart instantly ached to know if she had been violated by the wastrel Billington. How to ask? What to ask? Being a father was not an easy role to him, and now he had to fulfil it well with this his only legitimate child and daughter. Having removed her mother, the task of keeping her safe fell to him.

'Father, I did not expect to see you here!' she said as she steadied her horse.

'Obviously not, nor I you. So why are you here? Where is Whitaker? I understood her to be accompanying you at all times. The open road is no place for a young lady to be riding alone. Amelia, do you not realise the danger you place yourself in and the damage to your reputation if you are seen?' Wilson was being as polite as he could be, but his eyes were darting everywhere, looking into the trees to their right and over the field to their left.

'I wish to ride to town. I do not want that woman with me,' she snapped.

Her tone was not as it normally was. It had an edge to it that Wilson did not care for. 'So why is Whitaker not with you? And you both should be in a vehicle, not riding wild on horseback.'

'Because I want you to dismiss her for her arrogance! She has no knowledge regarding how to behave as a companion — or, for that matter, a decent house-keeper. She has a mouth like that of a tavern wench!' Amelia's colour, like her voice, was high.

'She is an excellent housekeeper, or I would not employ her. What do you know of tavern wenches? Neither should you have any such knowledge, Amelia. So why have you slipped free of her, and what have you been doing? The truth, no matter how base it is. I need to know, because as your father I will find out. Is this clandestine journey anything to do with a Mr Bartholomew Billington? If so, please tell me he has not convinced you to elope with him, like his last one.'

'Of course not, Father, but I will . . . What do you mean, his 'last one'?' Her head shot round and she stared into Wilson's eyes for the first time.

'The last woman whose reputation he destroyed — the last one — is what she is referred to as. She now languishes in a convent, placed there by her father until they discover if she is with child; and meanwhile he is free to find a keen and willing heart who has a purse attached to it to fall for his charms. Tell me it is not too late, Amelia!' Wilson could sense her guilt, and his heart felt like a vice had been placed around it and someone was slowly turning the screw. She was a pure heart, or had been, surviving Elizabeth's poison; and if that man had touched her and ruined her chance at finding a true love whom he approved of, he would take a stick to him or call the wimp out to a duel. Wilson's mind railed. He would take the fool down himself, the consequences of which he would answer for; or he would find passage to a new land before he was caught, taking Amelia and Nick with him. After all the loyalty his son and he had shown the country, they had been repaid by private mutterings of disgrace.

'No, it isn't. But he loves me. He . . . ' She started to weep.

'Dear, dear Amelia. Tell your father the truth of this situation; better to have a dented heart now than a ruined future because of him. I will take you home, where you will not receive any visitors until I return. I must finish my business with Nicholas. And I will not dismiss Whitaker. Whatever she said, I fear it was for your own good; but a servant dismissed without reference has a hard life to face, especially a woman.'

'He kissed me, Father. I believed him.' She turned her head away from him, her sense of shame obvious.

Wilson forced a smile and made her look at him, to calm her and mask his anger and disapproval. He did not want her feeling like a common whore in his or her eyes, but Billington's lips would feel the disapproval of Wilson's fist before he was a day older. 'A stolen kiss, no more, no less. Do not mention it again. Next time think more with your head and less with your heart.'

'Am I ruined, Father?'

'No, Amelia. A simple unseen kiss cannot ruin you if it was in private. But did it go beyond that? Are you still . . . ?' It was his turn to look away as he phrased his words carefully. 'Remember when you and Nick were children, seeing animals on the farm coupling . . . Did he . . . ?'

'Father! No! What do you think of me?' Tears welled up in her eyes and spilled down her cheeks. 'Will I have to return to Mama?' Her voice trembled.

'I think you are sweet and innocent, but men like him take delight in crushing such qualities and destroying the beauty I see in you. So you have been very fortunate. No, you will never have to live with your mother again. She has hurt and tainted our lives for too long already. Now I will see you safely home, and a message will be sent for Whitaker and your things, with our apologies for your quick change of plans.'

She nodded, and the two rode off in silence.

16

Nicholas entered the back of the butcher's and was greeted by a hefty-looking bald man with a raised cleaver. 'Good day to you, my friend,' Nicholas said calmly.

'Oh, I know who my friends are.' The man lowered the weapon.

'Perhaps; but one in need, Mr Gunnings, is a friend indeed, I have heard it said.'

'You may have, but I do not think I have mentioned being in need, sir. So state your business clearly, man, or be gone with you. I have no time for word games.'

'Very well. Mr Malachi G. Gunnings, you have a debt of five pounds and six shillings outstanding, do you not, and a man who holds your note?'

'How would you know that?' Malachi asked, his voice firm but low.

Nicholas saw instantly that Malachi did not want anyone else knowing his business. 'I am here as a friend, one who knows where the note is and can help you retrieve it and burn it. However, I need some information first.'

'What would that be?' The cleaver was discarded.

'I want to know where the body of Mr Thomas Henry Root would be taken by two ruffians in a barge.' Nicholas stared at him.

'Are you connected with the family?'

'I would like to see a man who is covering the death brought to justice, that is all.' He watched Malachi weigh his options up.

'If the man actually died, he would need to be seen by a doctor; and if he was known, his family would be notified. If a man with no family died, then he would be buried in a pauper's grave. However, if the men were rogues, then they could easily weigh a body down and sink it in the sea, so no one would be any the wiser. Now, I could guess which one happened, but that would be all I would be doing: guessing.'

'Do you know which? I believe you to

be an honest man.'

'You know I am.'

Nicholas nodded.

'I knew you would not let it go so easily. The man he was seeking and his friend are known at the Flagon Inn on the moor road. Crabton is one of them. He served in the navy. He was seen taking a pauper for burial, a fallen soldier who could not be saved. He'll be buried now. You can hardly dig the poor sod up. Let it be.'

'A man is dead and another is being used to take his place. Where is the constable?'

'You got my promissory note. Then I'll help you bring back the dead, but only if it gets Sands definitely off my back and frees up this town from his grip.'

'What does he want of you other than meat?'

'Favours for friends; information on folk. Costs me dear, he does. He uses people.'

'We have a deal, sir.' Nicholas offered his hand and was pleased when the man shook it in kind.

* * *

Wilson buried his fury deep and returned to meet Malachi and Nicholas as they were shutting up the shop for the day and about to leave.

Guy whispered, 'We burgled The Haven. He took stuff. I'm not for the transport. They'd skin me.' He was almost shaking.

'Ah, good for you, Nick.' Wilson ignored Guy.

'We need a constable, a warrant and a magistrate. Possibly another doctor — the young one I've heard of, if he is an honest sort,' Nicholas informed Wilson, his manner very relaxed.

Malachi nodded agreement. 'You have interesting friends, man,' he said.

'We will go to the constable. Malachi, can you bring Doctor Pearce? We have a body to identify, and word needs to be sent to the magistrate.'

Wilson looked at Nicholas. 'You have proof of this?'

'We have proof.' He pulled out the note with Gunning's name on it and showed it to him. His eyes looked keen to grab it.

Nicholas dropped it on the table in front of him. 'Take it. We are not blackmailers, and it is of no importance to me. I want a man whom I can trust with me, not one who is out to snatch back his debt.'

Malachi picked it up; he ripped it to shreds and then tossed it into the stove. It was no more; he was a free man again. 'Gentleman, to the Rabbit and Hare. Mr Penn, you know the constable. I will fetch the doctor.' He left them.

* * *

Nicholas and Wilson seated themselves on the settle opposite Jacob Battle. Guy was left watching the door to Dr Sands's to see if anyone came and went.

At first the man paid them no heed, seemingly lost in a permanent stupor over a tankard of ale. Then, as Nicholas placed a piece of paper in front of him — a note of debt to the value of ten pounds, the man's eyes widened and he went to grab it. Nicholas snatched it up. 'If you would like this back, then you have to listen to us. Send word to the magistrate and be prepared to testify to what you have found out about the events concerning the death of Mr Henry Root, and the burial of a 'pauper' whose name you will discover when you ascertain the true identity of the man who lies in The Haven as the miraculously lucky Thomas Henry Root.'

The man swallowed and nodded. 'I take no blame in this?' he asked, still looking at the paper.

'No, you will have been gathering facts for your investigation. We need to exhume the body; you see to the details and identify the man who is buried there. Then arrest Dr Sands. Have Dr Pearce stand in for now and oversee the welfare of the poor souls trapped in The Haven until the mess can be sorted out.'

The man smiled slowly. 'My pleasure.'

'Where is Billington?' Nicholas asked.

Jacob Battle looked upward. 'Building more debt. Losing more games.'

The two men stood up but did not leave the inn. Instead they went to a room above where a game of cards was being held.

Wilson entered and shouted, 'Mr

Bartholomew Billington — I come for the payment of this debt.' The paper he had been passed by Nicholas was in his hand.

Bartholomew stood, looking as though he might run from the room. He fumbled for words. The other men at the table cursed him for being a lowly debtor who could not pay for his losses. They hurriedly left the strangers to discuss arrangements.

Wilson strode over to Bartholomew and punched the man; he heard the nose break and watched him double up in agony. He had no chance to make up lies or excuses. 'That is from Miss Amelia Pendleton, whom you will never see again. You will spend some time in the debtors' gaol and then remove yourself from the county. Return north and stay away from my daughter, or we will have you locked up until the rats eat your toes.'

Billington made a bolt for the door. Nicholas punched him with one swift blow to the gut and left him where he fell. 'I will have him kept in the cellar until he can be collected and placed in the lock-up. The innkeeper will do it, I am sure.' He waved another piece of paper in the air.

'Did no one escape Sands's grasp?' Wilson asked.

'There are some ladies who I fear have been held to ransom over indiscreet love letters, and unpaid debts that they had hidden from their husbands or fathers. I will personally see they are returned.'

'You are becoming a regular saint,' Wilson quipped.

Nicholas's smile broadened. 'No, not that, not ever. But it is a good feeling to be looked upon as such, even temporarily.'

'How would I know?' Wilson said, and glanced at Nicholas. 'What of the key?' he asked.

'It was just like a miniature tap-room key. That was not a fanciful design, but as you realised the clue needed to find the lock it released. The treasure, whatever it was, must have been kept in a small barrel. It opened one in Root's manor and the one in the office of The Haven. Both had been made for the same home, but over time the property had been taken over by the Roots and the furniture moved to suit them. They had no knowledge of what they had all along. The first had nothing, so the second one had to hold the treasure, which Elizabeth had never disclosed.'

'But how did they know he had the key?' Wilson asked.

'I suspect that Root, the hapless chap, was caught as he tried to recover the jewels from The Haven. Perhaps a daring act to keep Amelia from harm's way to show her how much she could trust him and in so doing declaring his love for her. He bungled it and was chased by Sands's man. It was when the doctor saw him, and realised who he was, that another plan was hatched.' Nicholas placed his hand in his pocket and pulled out a velvet pouch on which was embroidered the initials *EB*. Inside was a diamond-and-sapphire pendant on a gold chain.

'He was another bungler, just like Bartholomew,' Wilson said. 'I shall find Amelia a man with a backbone.' He looked at the jewellery. 'This must be old. It could be worth a small fortune. Will you give it, as Elizabeth intended, to Amelia?'

Nicholas shook his head. 'That is for you to decide.'

Wilson looked thoughtful. 'Eventually, perhaps; but not for now, not just yet. She was foolish with the Billingtons, her head so easily turned at her first trusted freedom, and I have yet to decide who she takes after more, myself or her mother. Come — we have a case to close, and justice must be seen to be done. Then we can decide what we will do next.' He smiled.

Nicholas followed, collected Guy, and had to admit that the thought of not having anything to do next troubled him deeply. He, too, had been surprised by Amelia's actions, but then realised that she was no longer the girl whom he had once known so well. She had grown into a beautiful, headstrong woman, and somehow that naivety he had so wanted to protect had been slightly tarnished.

Time would reveal a new path for him to take, which would include Guy and Wilson no doubt. But what that would be, he did not know.

We do hope that you have enjoyed reading this large print book.

Did you know that all of our titles are available for purchase?

We publish a wide range of high quality large print books including:
Romances, Mysteries, Classics
General Fiction
Non Fiction and Westerns

Special interest titles available in large print are:
The Little Oxford Dictionary
Music Book, Song Book
Hymn Book, Service Book

Also available from us courtesy of Oxford University Press:
Young Readers' Dictionary
(large print edition)
Young Readers' Thesaurus
(large print edition)

For further information or a free brochure, please contact us at:
Ulverscroft Large Print Books Ltd.,
The Green, Bradgate Road, Anstey,
Leicester, LE7 7FU, England.
Tel: (00 44) **0116 236 4325**
Fax: (00 44) **0116 234 0205**